"Aren't you even a little curious to see where this might lead us?"

"No. We don't need to be led anywhere. We do great without kissing."

Caleb pulled her close and rested his cheek against the top of Melanie's head. His arms held her loosely. "You're right. We've always done great, you and me."

They had stood this way so many times before. But never quite like this. Today there was more. There was a tension, a new anticipation that hummed between them because now they knew what could happen if their lips met. Melanie both feared and reveled in the warring emotions.

Caleb raised his head and looked down into her emerald-green eyes.

"What are we doing, Caleb?"

"Are we supposed to know?"

"Shouldn't we?"

"Maybe. Or maybe we should just…"

He brushed his lips across hers.

Dear Reader,

We're smack in the middle of summer, which can only mean long, lazy days at the beach. And do we have some fantastic books for you to bring along! We begin this month with a new continuity, only in Special Edition, called THE PARKS EMPIRE, a tale of secrets and lies, love and revenge. And Laurie Paige opens the series with *Romancing the Enemy*. A schoolteacher who wants to avenge herself against the man who ruined her family decides to move next door to the man's son. But things don't go exactly as planned, as she finds herself falling…for the enemy.

Stella Bagwell continues her MEN OF THE WEST miniseries with *Her Texas Ranger,* in which an officer who's come home to investigate a murder fins complications in the form of the girl he loved in high school. Victoria Pade begins her NORTHBRIDGE NUPTIALS miniseries, revolving around a town famed for its weddings, with *Babies in the Bargain*. When a woman hoping to reunite with her estranged sister finds instead her widowed husband and her children, she winds up playing nanny to the whole crew. Can wife and mother be far behind? THE KENDRICKS OF CAMELOT by Christine Flynn concludes with *Prodigal Prince Charming,* in which a wealthy playboy tries to help a struggling caterer with her business and becomes much more than just her business partner in the process. Brand-new author Mary J. Forbes debuts with *A Forever Family,* featuring a single doctor dad and the woman he hires to work for him. And the men of the CHEROKEE ROSE miniseries by Janis Reams Hudson continues with *The Other Brother,* in which a woman who always contend her handsome neighbor as one of her best friends suddenly finds herself looking at him in a new light.

Happy reading! And come back next month for six new fabulous books, all from Silhouette Special Edition.

Gail Chasan
Senior Editor

Please address questions and book requests to:
Silhouette Reader Service
U.S.: 3010 Walden Ave., P.O. Box 1325, Buffalo, NY 14269
Canadian: P.O. Box 609, Fort Erie, Ont. L2A 5X3

The Other Brother

JANIS REAMS HUDSON

Silhouette®

SPECIAL EDITION®

Published by Silhouette Books

America's Publisher of Contemporary Romance

SILHOUETTE BOOKS

ISBN 0-373-24626-9

THE OTHER BROTHER

Copyright © 2004 by Janis Reams Hudson

This edition published by arrangement with Harlequin Books S.A.

® and TM are trademarks of Harlequin Books S.A., used under license. Trademarks indicated with ® are registered in the United States Patent and Trademark Office, the Canadian Trade Marks Office and in other countries.

Visit Silhouette Books at www.eHarlequin.com

Printed in U.S.A.

Books by Janis Reams Hudson

Silhouette Special Edition

Resist Me if You Can #1037
The Mother of His Son #1095
His Daughter's Laughter #1105
Until You #1210
*Their Other Mother #1267
*The Price of Honor #1332
*A Child on the Way #1349
*Daughter on His Doorstep #1434
*The Last Wilder #1474
†The Daddy Survey #1619
†The Other Brother #1626

*Wilders of Wyatt County
†Men of the Cherokee Rose

JANIS REAMS HUDSON

was born in California, grew up in Colorado, lived in Texas for a few years and now calls central Oklahoma home. She is the author of more than twenty-five novels, both contemporary and historical romances. Her books have appeared on the Waldenbooks, B. Dalton and BookRak bestseller lists and earned numerous awards, including the National Reader's Choice Award and Reviewer's Choice awards from *Romantic Times*. She is a three-time finalist for the coveted RITA® Award from Romance Writers of America and is a past president of RWA.

THE CHISHOLMS

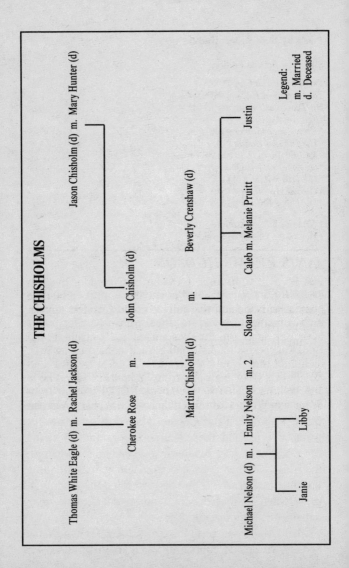

Thomas White Eagle (d) m. Rachel Jackson (d)

Jason Chisholm (d) m. Mary Hunter (d)

Cherokee Rose m.

John Chisholm (d)

Martin Chisholm (d)

Beverly Crenshaw (d) m.

Sloan   Caleb m. Melanie Pruitt   Justin

Michael Nelson (d) m. 1 Emily Nelson m. 2

Janie   Libby

Legend:
m. Married
d. Deceased

Chapter One

The fiddler's bow moved so fast it was little more than a blur beneath the gaily colored Chinese lanterns strung from barn to house and back again. Feet stomped, hands clapped, and couples whirled on the makeshift plywood dance floor. The winter wheat was in the ground, which was enough of a reason to party, but that wasn't what brought people to the Cherokee Rose ranch in central Oklahoma this early-October night. Cherokee Rose Chisholm's eldest grandson had taken a wife, and the celebration was in full swing. From farmers and ranchers to bankers to down-on-their-luck cowboys, people from all over the county, the state of Oklahoma and beyond filled the ranch yard to welcome Emily Nelson Chisholm and her two young daughters to the community.

There was even a rumor that a token Texan or two had shown up. Of course, to an Oklahoman, there was no such place as Texas. All that land south of the Red River was simply known as Baja Oklahoma.

Texans didn't like this description much, since they considered the area north of the Red River to be nothing more than North Texas. But what the heck. The annual Red River Rivalry, better known to the rest of the world as the Oklahoma University versus the University of Texas football game, was still two weeks away. For now, the Sooners would let the Longhorns drink their beer.

That beer was being tapped from the keg by Caleb Chisholm, the middle brother of Cherokee Rose's pride and joy—her three grandsons. Most people thought of Caleb as the quiet Chisholm. Sloan, the eldest, was outgoing and friendly, kindhearted and always ready to help someone in need. Justin, the youngest, had earned the nickname Wild Man back in high school; it was appropriate, and it had stuck. He liked to party, play practical jokes, and generally have a good time with the ladies.

But Caleb kept mostly to himself, when he wasn't trying to keep his two brothers from pounding on each other just for the fun of it. He was steady and dependable, and considered one of the best catches in the county, according to local beauty-shop gossip. He was a quiet man with a sober demeanor that added just a touch of mystery and made his rare smiles all the more powerful.

He flashed one of those rare smiles now as their nearest neighbor sashayed her way over to his keg of beer in time with the country band knocking them out from the front porch.

If anybody asked the three Chisholm brothers what kind of woman Melanie Pruitt was, three different answers would come back. She was a cute kid who didn't know what she really wanted; she wore her heart, usually broken, on her sleeve for all the world to see; and she was a tomboy who wouldn't think twice about playing along with, or even instigating, a good practical joke.

From her point of view, Caleb knew, Melanie considered herself none of those things, and all of them. She was right on both points. They'd known her all her life. She was the kid sister they'd never had. She'd been in love with Sloan, cried on Caleb's shoulder when that had proved to be all one-sided, and helped Justin egg the high school principal's house on Halloween.

As far as anyone in the Chisholm family was concerned, Mel was solid gold.

"Hey, Caleb. Some party." Her grin curved her mouth but did not reach the depths of those emerald-green eyes.

This troubled Caleb. Melanie had supposedly been over Sloan for a couple of years now. She had made friends with Emily, and encouraged Sloan to marry the woman. Now she came to the party held in honor of their marriage, and something was bothering her.

Her gaze strayed, and he followed it. She stared at Sloan and Emily as they two-stepped their way around the dance floor, laughing together as if they didn't have a care in the world. And to them, they didn't. Not this night, anyway.

"Dammit, Melanie," Caleb complained. "I thought you were over him."

Melanie blinked and looked up at Caleb. Twin lines formed between her eyes. "What? Who?"

"Who, hell. Sloan." It was all he could do to keep

from shaking her. "You were staring at him like you just lost your best friend."

Her eyes widened. "I was not. I wasn't even looking at him, much less thinking about him."

She seemed sincere enough, Caleb thought, but something was definitely troubling her. "If it's not Sloan, then what's wrong?"

Melanie shook her head. "It's nothing."

"Come on, Melanie. This is me you're talking to."

"Okay, I'll rephrase. It's nothing I want to talk about, but it has nothing to do with Sloan. You know better than that, or you should."

He shrugged. "I thought I did. You're sure you're over him?"

She narrowed those deep green eyes at him. "You're going to make me mad, you keep asking that. I've been over him for years. And even if I wasn't, look at them." She waved a hand toward Sloan and Emily on the dance floor. The tall, dark-skinned man and the small golden-haired woman danced and gazed at each other as if they were the only two people in the world. "Even a blind person can see how perfect they are together, how much in love they are. And, Caleb?"

"Yeah?"

"I'm not blind."

"Got it. Consider me sufficiently chastised."

Her lips quirked. "That'll be the day."

"Uncle Caleb, Uncle Caleb, look at us!"

The cry came from little Libby, Emily's six-year-old daughter. She and her eight-year-old sister, Janie, were both being whirled around the dance floor by Justin, Caleb and Sloan's youngest brother. At their begging, Justin had been teaching the girls to two-step for the past week. They had wanted to be ready for the party.

"Look, Uncle Caleb!" Janie called.

Uncle. Damn if Caleb didn't get a great big kick out of that. He couldn't help but grin. "I see," he called back. "Looking good, ladies."

"Look at them," Melanie said, clearly delighted. "Inside of a month he'll have them doing the Cotton-Eyed Joe and the schottische."

Caleb laughed. "Month, nothing. Those two are quick. They've already just about got the Cotton-Eyed Joe down pat."

"You're getting a kick out of this uncle thing, aren't you?" Melanie asked.

"You better believe it," he said. "They're angels, both of them."

"Oh, look." Melanie pointed across the dance floor. "There goes your grandmother, with the Methodist minister."

"Grandmother loves to dance," he said.

"So do you," Melanie said. "Why aren't you out there?"

"I'm on beer duty."

"To heck with that. We can get our own beer. Besides, barracuda at twelve o'clock. Bearing down on you with a gleam in her eyes. You're going to want to dance with me. And I mean right now."

Caleb started to turn around to see what she was talking about, but she grabbed his arm and started dragging him toward the dance floor.

"Don't look," she hissed. "It's Alyshia Campbell."

"Enough said." Caleb took her right hand in his left, put his right hand on her waist and spun her into a fast two-step amid the other dancers.

Caleb shuddered. Alyshia Campbell, aka the barracuda, aka the shark, the piranha, the pariah and a dozen other names that weren't so nice. Alyshia knew about all the names people called her. She enjoyed her nasty reputation.

She was older than Caleb's thirty-three by at least ten years, and she was married to the local used-car salesman who happily turned a blind eye to his wife's numerous boyfriends while she turned a blind eye to his. A person couldn't talk about Alyshia or Jerry Campbell without getting a bad taste in the mouth. And for some reason, Alyshia had apparently decided Caleb was going to be her next conquest, although word was that she hadn't dumped her current one yet.

"Thanks," he said to Melanie with feeling. "I owe you one."

Melanie shook her shoulder-length hair back and laughed. "You better believe you do."

Caleb arched a brow. "Are you saying that dancing with me is a hardship?"

"Of course not. You know you're one of the best dancers around. But I saved your bacon, pal. For that, you owe me."

"Looks like your rescue was short-lived. Here she comes."

Melanie glanced over her shoulder and saw Alyshia bearing down on them with a predatory smile on her surgically enhanced face.

"May I cut in?" Alyshia purred.

Melanie smiled. Caleb had never seen that particular look on Melanie's face before. For a moment, he wondered which woman was the more dangerous. Then he shook off the feeling. This was Melanie, his friend.

"Go away, Alyshia," Melanie said dismissively. "This one's taken." Without missing a beat, Melanie slid her hands to the back of Caleb's head and pulled him down to meet her mouth.

The shock was instantaneous. A sharp jolt of electricity. Intense heat, flames licking from the inside out. Arousal, hard and fast. The air turned hot and heavy, and with it, Caleb thought that if Melanie wasn't feeling what he was feeling, his life would never be complete.

Startled, he tore his mouth from hers and stared.

Melanie blinked up at him, her breath rasping. "Oh…my…God."

Caleb swallowed. "Uh, yeah." He swallowed again. "That was…"

She swallowed. "Yeah."

"Come on, you two." Alyshia smirked. "Get a room, for heaven's sake."

Caleb and Melanie both ignored her.

Alyshia shrugged and walked away.

"What just happened?" Melanie asked, a dazed look in her eyes.

"I…I don't know. An explosion, I think."

Around them friends and neighbors swirled across the dance floor, feet stomped, voices laughed, the band blared.

"Yeah." Melanie looked away, around, anywhere but at Caleb. She couldn't believe what had just happened. "Yeah. That would explain it."

They stared at each other another long moment, then Caleb looked away and shuffled his feet. "Anyway, uh, thanks. For getting Alyshia off my back, I mean."

"Hey," Melanie said with a big fake smile. "What are friends for? Oh, look, there's Daddy. See you later." She escaped Caleb and the dance floor so fast, she was pretty sure she left a vacuum in her wake.

What else could a woman do when she'd just done the unthinkable and kissed her best friend? And not just kissed, but *Kissed*.

It wasn't her fault, she told herself. That lightning bolt from the sky shouldn't have happened. The kiss had been meant as a joke. A ploy to get rid of Alyshia. A teasing gesture between friends. Not...not...not fireworks.

"What's the matter with you?" her father groused. "You look like you just got thrown by a wild bronc."

Leave it to her father to describe perfectly what she was feeling. "Uh, no," she managed. "Just a fast whirl on the dance floor."

He patted her on the shoulder. "Well, you have a good time, little girl. I'll find you later."

"Daddy," she said as he turned to walk away.

Ralph Pruitt stopped and looked back at his only child. "Yeah?"

Melanie opened her mouth, then closed it and shook her head. "Nothing. I'll find you when I'm ready to go home."

As he walked away, she bit the end of her tongue to keep from calling out a warning to him: *No gambling*.

Maybe she was getting wiser, keeping her mouth shut this time. Lord knew the warning would have fallen on deaf ears. Gambling was an addiction with her father. He used to go to meetings up in Oklahoma City, and the people there, fellow compulsive gamblers, had been a help. But when Melanie's mother left them a couple of years ago, Ralph had given up the meetings. He'd been gambling ever since.

Call her a cynic, but if her father would win his bets more often she wouldn't worry so much. But Lady Luck favored Ralph Pruitt only often enough to keep him coming back. His losses were mounting, and the ranch finances were hurting because of it. It was that, rather than any upset over Sloan's marriage, that had been troubling Melanie when Caleb had questioned her earlier.

Now, in addition to worrying about her father and the ranch, and wondering what her mother was up to, there was that kiss to torment her. She ought to be able to laugh it off and forget it, but for now it loomed large in her mind.

By 3:00 a.m. that damn kiss still occupied Melanie's mind. It filled every nook and cranny and wouldn't let her sleep. She had tossed and turned so much that her bed looked like a disaster zone. By sunup, so did she.

She did her best with a cold shower and makeup, but nothing could disguise the sleepless night she'd just spent.

Her father obviously noticed, if the sudden height of his eyebrows was any indication, but, with uncharacteristic wisdom, he said nothing as he drove the two of them to church.

For as long as Melanie could remember, her father had driven the family to church every Sunday morning. Only calving or foaling could keep him home, and neither of those was taking place this day. Still, it seemed odd that it was only the two of them in the pickup, though it had been just the two of them for more than two years now, since Melanie's mother had left them.

She should be here, Melanie thought. Her mother should be here with them on the way to church. She shouldn't be off in sunny Arizona living the high life. And sending the bills home for the ranch to pay her expenses. Mounting expenses.

Between her mother and father, Melanie was about ready to bang her head against the nearest wall, financially speaking.

Patience. She would pray for patience. If she was very, very good, maybe God would grant her some.

But first, she thought as she and her father entered the church, she would pray to become invisible. How was she supposed to sit in church and concentrate on the sermon with Caleb Chisholm just across the aisle?

She did her best to focus on the minister, her bible, her hymnal, each in turn. She must have managed to keep last night's kiss from her mind, because lightning did not shoot through the roof of the sanctuary and strike her dead for having lascivious thoughts in church.

After the final amen was delivered and announcements were made, Melanie managed to fumble long enough with her purse and her bible and trading small talk with the pharmacist seated next to her to allow plenty of time for the Chisholms to get halfway down the aisle before her father finally took her by the arm and dragged her from the pew.

"What's the matter with you today?" he grumbled. "You're slow as molasses."

She dragged her feet and slowed even more. "What's the hurry?"

"Maybe I'm hungry."

That was the other part of their Sunday ritual—dinner out after church at Lucille's Café on Main. Her father would order the chicken-fried steak, and, because Melanie made pets out of her laying hens and refused to butcher them, she would have fried chicken—someone else's fried chicken, thank you very much.

With great relief, or so she told herself, Melanie noted that when she and her father finally exited the church the Chisholms were already pulling out of the parking lot. There were so many of them now that Sloan had a wife and two new stepdaughters that it took them two vehicles to haul everyone.

At her side she heard her father mutter a curse.

"What's the matter with you today?" she demanded, parroting his words. "You're grumpy as a bear with a sore paw."

"I told you," he said tersely, nudging her none too gently down the church steps. "I'm hungry."

"Well, by all means, then," she said with exaggerated sweetness. "Let's feed you."

The town of Rose Rock had a population of just under two thousand, but it boasted three cafés, a steak house, a pizza parlor, two hamburger joints and a hot-dog stand. Nearly every seat in every one of them filled up fast at noon each Sunday.

If all the churches were to let out at the same time, it would be a disaster. People would be lined up all the way up and down Main waiting for a table. But while the Methodists, the Baptists, the Presbyterians and the First Christians all let out at noon, the Baptists, the Southern Baptists, Church of Christ and the small congregation of Latter-day Saints never let out before twelve-thirty. Melanie didn't know if that was because they were all so naughty during the week that it took them longer to make up for it, or if their preachers were simply long-winded. In any case, she thought as she and her father stepped through the front door of Lucille's, it was one very practical reason to be glad she was a Baptist.

Even then, it was a near thing finding a table, but Melanie spotted one that thankfully was not too close to where the Chisholms had pushed three tables together in the middle of the room. The only drawback was that she would have to pass their table to get to the empty one.

She was being stupid, she knew, shying away from Caleb this way. They saw each other every Sunday, and usually a time or two more during the week. All she had to do was nod and smile—at the whole family, not just Caleb—and move right along. Simple. Easy. No problem at all.

Except that just as she was managing it and stepping past their table, her father placed his hand on her shoulder.

"Hold up a minute," he told her.

He stood beside the Chisholms' table and greeted them, leaving Melanie no choice but to face them.

"Rose," Ralph said to the matriarch of the Chisholm clan. "You sure know how to throw a party."

"Thank you, Ralph." Cherokee Rose Chisholm smiled. "It's not every day one of my grandsons gets married."

"Some of us," he said, casting a dark look at Melanie, "are still waiting for our *children* to marry and *produce* grandchildren."

Carefully avoiding looking at Caleb, Melanie leaned down and batted her eyes at Justin. "Are you busy tonight? My daddy wants me to get married and have children."

Justin screwed up his face in concentration, then smiled. "I've got a date tonight, but tomorrow night's Billy Ray's birthday, and I'm supposed to pick you up at seven. We wouldn't be able to get married since we don't have a license or anything, but we could probably get started on the kids after the party.''

The adults at the table laughed. Emily, Justin's new sister-in-law, gave him that frown she used on her daughters when they'd been naughty. "Justin, shame."

Melanie quirked her lips and pinched the end of Justin's nose. "In your dreams, fella."

Justin heaved a big sigh. "Yeah, you're right. Besides, it'd be like kissing my sister."

Melanie turned to her father and shrugged. "Sorry, Daddy. Looks like I'll be staying single a little while longer."

Ralph Pruitt huffed out a breath of mock disgust at their play, and at the laughter around the table. "Well, then, the least he can do is give you a ride home. I've got an errand to run in the opposite direction, and I need to leave now. Y'all don't mind, do you?" he asked the table at large.

"Now wait a min—"

But Melanie's protest was cut off by Rose's voice. "Of course we don't mind. You know you don't even have to ask."

"Yeah," Sloan said. "Come on, Mel, pull up a chair."

Melanie gaped at her father. He was fobbing her off on the Chisholms like she was a stray dog. An unwanted stray dog, at that. "Daddy…"

He gave her a peck on the cheek and a pat on the back. "There you go, little girl. I won't be home till late, so don't wait up for me. Afternoon, y'all." He tipped his hat and walked away, leaving Melanie standing there feeling as if she'd just been betrayed.

"Daddy," she called after him, but to no avail. Her

father walked straight to the door and out without a backward glance.

Inside, over and around the embarrassment he'd just caused her by foisting her onto the neighbors, fury burned. If he was, indeed, going in the opposite direction from home, that meant he was headed in the general direction of Oklahoma City.

There were no horses running at Remington Park today, but there were a hundred other places he could go to gamble, not the least of which was any one of several dozen tribal casinos around the state. Damn his hide.

"Come on," Sloan told her. "Join us, Mel."

She turned to face the table. There was one empty chair. It was between Justin and Caleb. Terrific. But there was no way around it, so she stifled a sigh and sat down.

"Thanks," she said to the table at large. "For letting me barge in on your Sunday dinner."

"Nonsense," Rose said matter-of-factly. "If you came through the front door in the middle of the night, you wouldn't be barging in. Not with us. Hello, Donna," Rose added to the waitress who came to take their orders. "Melanie has joined us. She'll be needing something to drink."

The meal with the Chisholms was not the ordeal Melanie had feared it would be, seated next to Caleb as she was. He and everyone else treated her as they always had—as one of the family. There was no hint that her father's behavior had seemed, if not rude, then at least odd. There was no hint from Caleb or anyone that anything momentous had happened on that make-shift dance floor the night before.

As the meal progressed, Melanie finally began to relax. She had simply been overreacting, that was all. And what a relief it was to realize that. She had kissed a friend as a joke, to rescue him from a potentially sticky situation. That was all there had been to it. Whatever she had thought she'd felt had merely been a trick of her obviously overactive imagination.

And surely the sly looks that passed between Sloan and Justin had nothing to do with her. Again, only her imagination working overtime.

It was not her imagination, however, that had her standing alone with Caleb beside his pickup as the rest of the Chisholms piled into Rose's SUV and drove away. And those twin smirks from Caleb's brothers were not her imagination, either.

"Well," Caleb said, "that was subtle."

"As a Mack truck," Melanie said in agreement. "I'm sorry you got stuck with taxi duty."

"Hey, forget it." He walked around to the passenger side and unlocked the door for her. "What are friends for?"

The instant the words were out of his mouth, they both wished he hadn't said them. Both pretended he hadn't. Pretended they didn't recall Melanie uttering those very words on the dance floor the night before, right after…well, right after the big disaster.

Melanie averted her gaze and jumped into the pickup.

Caleb silently cursed himself with every step he took around the pickup to the driver's door. He cursed his brothers. He cursed Ralph Pruitt. He cursed Alyshia Campbell.

But most of all, he cursed himself, for reminding them both of something that shouldn't have affected them in the least, but had somehow altered the universe.

Melanie had been so uncomfortable when her father had stopped her beside their table that she had looked everywhere but at him. But eventually, as the meal progressed, her stiffness had eased. Her smile had come more easily. Her laughter had sounded more natural. She had even managed to look at him a time or two. Out the corner of her eye. When she thought he wasn't looking.

Now she was all pokered up again.

With a heavy sigh, he climbed in behind the wheel and started the engine. He hadn't a clue what to say to her, but surely at some point during the twenty-minute drive to her house he could come up with something. Something that had nothing to do with his having lain awake last night giving serious thought to figuring out a way to kiss her again.

The very idea appalled him. He had always valued Melanie's friendship. He had no intention of ruining that simply because his glands decided to act up. True, lifelong friends were hard to come by.

Besides which, this particular lifelong friend would likely box his ears if he tried kissing her again.

He was an imbecile. That was all there was to it. They were friends. Just friends. She hadn't meant anything by that kiss any more than he had. It had been a joke, that was all. A prank. God knew Mel loved a good prank.

It was too quiet in the pickup, road and wind noise notwithstanding. Deciding a little music might help break the tension, Caleb reached for the radio knob on his dash.

Melanie must have had the same idea at the same

time; their hands collided over the knob. For a brief instant their fingers ended up entwined. A sharp tingling sensation raced up Caleb's arm and he jerked.

Melanie must have felt it, too, he thought, since she jerked away every bit as fast as he did.

"Sorry," she muttered, using her other hand to rub her arm, further convincing him she suffered the same sharp tingling sensation.

At least he wasn't alone in this, he thought. And he hadn't been alone in his reaction last night, either. But that didn't give him any insight into how to deal with the situation. Ignore it? Act like nothing had happened? Say something about it? Kiss her again.

"Melanie," he began, with no clue as to what he was going to say next.

"I thought you were going to turn on the radio." Her voice was sharp, terse, as she folded her arms across her chest and stared out the windshield.

"Yeah. Sure." Okay, he thought. She didn't want to talk. He turned on the radio. Neither spoke again.

When Caleb turned off the highway onto the gravel lane that led to Melanie's house—essentially her driveway, but too long to be called by that name—he had to slow the pickup to a crawl. The gravel had long since disappeared, leaving bare clay, baked in the Oklahoma sun to the consistency of solid granite. The ruts were deep and many. In more than one spot he had to veer to keep from scraping his undercarriage, some of the ruts were so deep.

What the hell were she and her father thinking, letting this road get in such bad shape? They should have taken the box blade to it before it had completely dried after the last rain and smoothed it out. Then they should have hauled in a load of gravel.

He glanced over at Melanie, but her shoulders were set so hard against him he figured that if he said anything his voice would just bounce right off her, so he kept his mouth shut and bounced his way toward her house.

Chapter Two

It had been the longest ride of Melanie's life. The only saving grace had been that Caleb didn't bring up the kiss.

She didn't know whether to be grateful or angry. She supposed she was a little of both, she thought as she watched his taillights disappear down the driveway in a cloud of dust. Grateful that she'd escaped having to talk about something that she didn't understand, something that embarrassed her to the core, and angry with both of them for not bringing it out in the open so they could put themselves and their friendship back on an even keel.

Shaking her head, Melanie trudged to her bedroom to change into work clothes. Since her father wasn't home, the remainder of the day's chores fell to her.

She didn't mind the work. In fact, she loved each and every chore—well, okay, maybe she didn't love each one, but she couldn't think of a single chore she actually hated. Except on the rare occasion when an animal had to be put down. And housework. She hated anything that hinted of housework.

Other than that, she didn't mind the effort it took to keep a ranch running. It was good honest work. It made a person stronger, and not just physically. What she did mind was having to do her father's share so he could run around losing money all over the damn territory.

She would start with the most important chores and work her way down until dark. The most important were the mares. There were three of them, and they were her star boarders.

Well, Melanie thought with a chuckle, they were her only boarders. Their owners paid extra to make sure their beauties were well taken care of, including being stabled each night so they wouldn't have to spend the nights out in the open.

If given a choice, nearly all of Pruitt Ranch's own horses would stand outside in a blizzard and let icicles form on their muzzles before they would willingly step a single hoof inside a barn. PR horses were an independent lot.

At the back door, in the kitchen, Melanie stomped her feet into her boots and headed out. She juggled the list of chores in her mind. It wasn't fair to the mares to bring then in from the paddock and lock them up in the barn in the middle of the day just because she wanted to take her list of chores in some particular order.

But part and parcel with putting them up for the night was cleaning out their stalls, so she started there. After that she drained the water trough in the corral and gave it a good scrubbing. Ever since the West Nile virus made its appearance in Oklahoma she tried not to let water stand in the troughs, or anywhere else, for more than a couple of days. Lord knew there were enough natural breeding places for mosquitoes; she wasn't about to provide more if she could help it.

By the time she did a few more chores, drove out to the back pasture and checked on the cattle there, then came back and stabled the mares, it was nearly dark. While she was brushing down the last mare she heard a vehicle rumble up to the barn on the other side of the corral.

It was her dad. She recognized the sound of his pickup. After the way he'd dumped her at the café earlier, she wasn't sure she was ready yet to talk to him. She took her time with the last mare.

Finally, she could delay no longer. In the deep twilight she walked the fifty yards from the barn to the back door and entered the house.

Her father was on the phone. As she came in, he said, "I told you I'd get you the money."

Melanie's stomach clenched. She froze in the open doorway.

Her father hung up the phone and turned toward the refrigerator. "What's for supper?"

For one long moment, Melanie could do no more than gape. When she didn't answer, her father turned to look at her. She snapped. Somehow, behind her, the door slammed shut.

"Maybe if you'd eaten dinner after church this afternoon you wouldn't be hungry."

"Hmmph." He appeared unimpressed with her sudden anger. "You ate, and I'll bet you're hungry."

"Bet?" It was all she could do to keep from shrieking. "Haven't you placed enough *bets* for one day?"

A flush of guilty red stained his cheeks. He turned back toward the fridge and pulled open the door. "I don't know what you're talking about."

"You don't, huh?" She jammed the heel of one boot into the bootjack and worked her foot free. "Then who was that on the phone that you were promising money to?"

His shoulders stiffened, but he didn't turn to face her. "None of your business."

"Oh, it's my business, all right." She took off her second boot and stalked across the room to grab his arm and tug him around. "You've been taking money out of the ranch account for months like you think we've got our own printing press."

Melanie stopped and took a deep breath. This was the man who played horsey while she rode his shoulders. The man who taught her to ride a real horse, gave her her first pony, taught her to rope a steer. Taught her to love the land. Taught her what it was to love family.

"Daddy, I love you, but this has to stop before you bankrupt us."

"Aw, don't give me that," he said, pained. "It hasn't been that bad."

"Hasn't been that bad?" Her voice rose in pitch as she waved her arms. "Look around. Do you think we let the hands go three weeks ago because we didn't need them anymore? Because we like working ourselves half to death and never catching up?"

"I know you said we were short," Ralph said, "but that was before we sold the calves. We're fine now."

"We might be," she said, "if we hadn't been in the

red before the sale, thanks to your gambling and Mama's credit card charges.''

Fayrene and Ralph Pruitt had been separated for nearly two years. Not legally, on paper, but physically. One day Fayrene had decided she was tired of Ralph paying more attention to his cattle and horses—even his pickup—than her. She had packed a bag and hauled tail to Phoenix to live with her sister. She called every couple of weeks to talk to Melanie, but never Ralph.

There had never been a discussion about how Fayrene was to support herself. She had the same credit card she'd always carried, in the name of the ranch; Ralph had never asked her to give it back or stop using it. As long as she was his wife, she was entitled, he said.

It was Melanie, however, who had to figure out how to pay the mounting bills.

"I'm telling you, Daddy, we won't make it through the winter at this rate. What are we supposed to do, sell off land? Or maybe Big Angus.''

"We're not selling so much as an acre of the PR, and we're damn sure not selling Big Angus.''

Big Angus was the enormous bull that was the foundation of their breeding program. His championship bloodline, not to mention his perfect confirmation, made him one of the most valuable bulls in the state.

"You sound just like your mother," Ralph went on, "always exaggerating, making things sound worse than they are.''

"Daddy—''

"I'm hungry. Do we still have any of that roast beef? We can have sandwiches.''

And that, Melanie knew from past experience, was the end of any discussion on money.

* * *

Melanie had been right about the end of any more money talk with her father. He stuffed two thick roast beef sandwiches, one after the other, into his mouth then kissed her on top of her head and went to bed.

Monday morning she faced the chores alone again. Instead of her father, in the kitchen making coffee as he did most mornings, she found a note:

Gone to the city. Don't wait up.

He meant Oklahoma City. If he'd been going to Rose Rock, he'd have said he was gone to town. In Oklahoma, there was generally only one "city," and that was Oklahoma City. Tulsa was Tulsa; everything else was called by its name unless you lived in the country and were referring to the nearest town, then it was "town." But "the city" was Oklahoma City.

There was legitimate ranch business he could take care of in the city. The big tractor-supply places were there, and they needed a new part. But he usually had the parts store in town order whatever he needed.

He was up to no good again. Gambling. There was no other logical explanation for this latest disappearing act.

Melanie was so angry, so frustrated, she wished heartily for a punching bag. Or a cord of wood to chop. Since neither of those was handy, she bit down on her emotions and turned the mares out for the day. She found little satisfaction in mucking out their stalls, but it had to be done.

When she went to the feed room in the back of the barn, she swore. Her father was supposed to have brought home a new load of sweet feed for the mares two days ago. Obviously he'd had more important things on his mind, because there were no new bags.

She should wait until later, after she'd put in another few hours of work, but maybe the trip to the feed store in town would settle her down. Between anger at her father, and the dream she'd had of kissing Caleb, she felt ready to explode. Mucking out stalls had not helped.

She drove to town, cursing herself for postponing her work, knowing that she would have to stop early enough that evening to get ready to go with Justin to the birthday party. Maybe she would drown her sorrows in beer. Except she never got drunk. She wasn't much of a drinker at all. She was a sipper. It took her all night to get through two glasses of beer. If she was drinking bottles or cans, she couldn't finish two unless she stayed up all night to get the job done. Still, she was looking forward to the evening.

What she was not looking forward to, she thought as she stopped at the mailbox at the end of her driveway on her way back from the feed store, was opening the mail. It was, as usual, all bills. No prize patrol, no letter from Ed McMahon waiting to tell her she'd won a million dollars. Just another bill from the electric company, who, for some reason, expected money from them about this time every month. An insurance statement. An invoice from the credit card company. That was going to hurt.

And hurt, it did. She put off opening it for as long as she could. She unloaded the sweet feed. She made sure the bags were stacked straight. She straightened up the rest of the storage room. She went to the house and made herself another roast beef sandwich. She would be glad to see the last of that roast; she was getting tired of it, no matter how good it tasted.

Then there was nothing legitimate standing between her and the bills. With grim resolve, she carried them to the desk in the small den off the living room and grabbed the letter opener. As if about to take a dose of particularly foul-tasting medicine, she held her breath and opened the worst of them—the credit card bill— first.

She nearly staggered at the amount due. Good grief! Last month she had paid off the entire balance, and now the account was completely maxed out. All five digits of the allowable amount. What the— In *one month?*

''Mama, what have you done?''

The list of charges was as long as her arm and took up two pages. None was for less than five hundred dollars. Department stores—high-end ones. Victoria's Secret? What could her *mother* have bought *there* for six-hundred-fifty-seven dollars? There were other places listed, whose merchandise or services Melanie could only guess at.

The charge that stopped her heart was from a Scotts-dale clinic for more than ten thousand dollars.

Oh, God. A clinic? Her mother was ill. How serious was it? It must be bad to cost that much. Why hadn't Mama called to tell them?

She reached for the phone with trembling hands and dialed her mother's number in Arizona. She got the damn answering machine.

''Mama, it's Melanie. Are you there? If you're there pick up. I just got the credit card bill. Mama, what's wrong? Are you sick? Hurt? What's happened? All that money charged to the clinic. Why didn't you let the insurance cover it? Please call. You've got me terrified here. Call. And hurry, Mama.''

A sick feeling bubbled in the pit of Melanie's stomach. Oh, God. Her mother was sick, and the Pruitt Ranch was in big financial trouble. Heaven help her, there was no way she could pay off the credit card balance this time. And with interest rates that would do a loan shark proud, it was going to take years to pay off.

And how could she even consider worrying about such a trivial matter as that when for all she knew her mother could be dying?

Melanie sat heavily and buried her face in her hands. What was she going to do? How could she help her mother? She had to assume that if her mother was in a really bad way she would have called. Or Aunt Karen would have. But nobody ran up a ten-thousand-dollar tab at a clinic for a hangnail or a bout with the flu.

And why, oh why, hadn't she used their health insurance instead of charging it all to the credit card? Had she lost her mind?

She was obviously feeling well enough to buy out half of the finer shops in Phoenix, whose charges were dated after the charge at the clinic. That was something, then.

If her mother's health weren't enough, Melanie felt as if the very survival of the PR rested on her shoulders. In truth, it did. Her parents certainly weren't helping. They were, in fact, the problem. Both of them.

She loved her parents deeply, but right now all she wanted to do was knock their heads together. They had to stop this. She had to make them stop.

But how? She had tried talking, begging, demanding. Nothing had worked. What else could she do? She couldn't sit around and let them take the ranch under. She knew they didn't want the ranch to go under any more than she did, it was just that they had both become as irresponsible as a couple of teenagers since Mama had moved out. She supposed she should be grateful they'd...

That was it. She didn't have to convince them of anything. When her parents had separated they had agreed that they wanted to ensure that if anything happened to one of them, Melanie would still have the ranch. They'd had their lawyer draw up papers giving Melanie fifty percent of the ranch, with twenty-five percent going to each of her parents. Unless the two of them joined forces—an event not likely to happen in the foreseeable future—control rested in Melanie's hands. It was time she exercised it.

She reached for the phone.

Thirty minutes later it was done. They weren't out of debt, weren't going to be for a good long while. But neither of her parents would be able to add to the problem. She had closed the credit card account and canceled the ATM cards. No one could charge anything to the ranch, except at the feed store in town, and no one could withdraw cash from the bank without writing a check. And she had the only checkbook. If her mother's health caused more expenses Melanie would handle it. Somehow.

Heaven help her, her mother and father were going to hit the roof when they found out what she'd done.

She wished her actions made her feel better but they didn't. That sick feeling still rumbled in her stomach. Who was she to tell her parents what to do? They had worked hard all their lives, built this ranch up from the small, one-man operation Grandpa had left Daddy.

They were her *parents,* and she was treating them like children, taking control of their money, cutting them off.

Heaven help her.

Billy Ray's birthday celebration that night at the Road Hog Saloon was, by all accounts, a rousing success.

By all accounts except Melanie's. She was most definitely not enjoying herself. Her beer kept disappearing right out of her glass. She reached for the pitcher on the table to give herself a refill, but, oh, great. The pitcher was empty.

"More beer!" she yelled. But the band was so loud, she doubted anyone heard her. It was a local group called the Aloha Shirt Boys, named for the shirts they wore, not the music they played; they played country and western, with a little Cajun thrown in now and then, and they played it loud. L-O-U-D loud.

"More beer!" she yelled again, pounding the pitcher on the table. Why wasn't there any more beer?

"Hey, sweetcakes." Her buddy, Justin, slid in next to her in the booth. "Whatcha hollering about?" He had picked her up at seven, as planned, and they had driven to the Road Hog for Billy Ray's party, both grateful that whoever had done the choosing had chosen the Road Hog over Deuces at the other end of town. If the Road Hog was a dump, Deuces was three notches below a dive.

"I'm outta beer." She frowned at her empty glass, the empty pitcher, then at Justin. Her pal. Caleb's brother. Caleb, with the magic lips.

No, no, no. Mustn't think about Caleb's lips. Nope. Bad lips. Shame on those lips. No more lips for her, by golly. She shouldn't even be thinking about lips, but she needed lips to drink her beer.

"I'm outta beer," she said again.

It was easier to think about beer. If she just kept thinking about it, pouring it down her throat, she wouldn't have to think about Caleb's lips. Or her father. Or her mother's health. Now *there* was a subject to get a girl to drinking.

Her father didn't yet know what she'd done, but she had called her mother back and left a second message, warning her not to use the credit card because it would be turned down.

Oh, boy, howdy, that was going to go over like a lead balloon.

They were going to hate her. Mama and Daddy were both going to hate her for this.

"I want more beer."

Good grief, was that her voice? That ugly, whiny sound?

Her parents weren't here. And neither were Caleb's lips. She was safe for now.

"Where you been?" she demanded of Justin. "This's the firs' I've seen you since we got here."

Justin hooted. "Sweetcakes, did you know your words are slurring?"

She blinked and opened her eyes wide. "Are not."

"Are too."

"Tha's a lie."

Justin hooted again. "You're drunk as a skunk. How much beer have you had?"

"This is her third pitcher." The waitress, Linda, clunked down a fresh pitcher of beer and whipped the empty one away.

Justin goggled. "Third? What's the deal, Mel? You never drink this much."

Using two hands to make sure she didn't spill a drop, Melanie refilled her parched glass, then guzzled the entire contents to soothe her parched throat.

"Ah." She slapped the glass back down onto the table and smacked her lips. "Tha's better."

Justin was starting to get worried. This wasn't like Mel at all. She never drank this much, and she damn sure never guzzled a full glass in one gulp. "Three pitchers?"

"'S a lie."

"Come on, pal, what's going on? It's me, here. You can tell me anything, you know that."

"Nope." She shook her head and refilled her glass yet again. "You're my fun pal. Caleb's my talkin'-to pal."

"You want me to call Caleb?"

Her eyes nearly popped out of her head. "Lips?"

Justin burst out laughing.

"No way, José." She shook her head so hard she nearly fell against him. "*He's* part of the prob— The prol— The damn reason. Him and his lips." She snorted. "His lips, my parents. Either one would be enough to send a girl to the nearest bar, and I've got 'em both to deal with."

The way Mel was glaring at him, as though Caleb and his lips and her parents, whatever they had to do with anything, were somehow *his* fault, had Justin swallowing back another burst of laughter. Sober, she was capable of giving him a black eye if he made her too mad. He had no idea what she might do when drunk, because he'd never seen her like this before. He didn't know how to deal with this Mel.

"You hold that thought, sweetcakes." He patted her on the shoulder. "I'll be back in a minute."

"I don' thin' so."

Halfway out of the booth, Justin paused and looked back at her. "You don't think I'll be back?"

"Nope." She took a sip of beer and smacked her lips.

"Why not?"

"'Cuz Blaire Harding just walked in, an' I happen to know you've got a *baaad* case of the hots for her."

At the mention of Blaire Harding's name, Justin's head whipped around all on its own. Without direction from his brain, his eyes scanned, then zeroed in on her as if they were laser-guided. Without looking back, he slid from the booth.

"See ya, kid," he said over his shoulder. Because Mel was right. He had a *baaad* case of the hots for Blaire Harding, and the woman had been avoiding him like the plague for days.

But before he got too carried away, he made his way outside—where he could make sure Blaire didn't leave before he had a chance to drool—er, talk to her. The noise level was slightly lower outside than in, which was his reason for going there. He unclipped his cell phone from his belt and called Caleb.

Caleb pulled into the gravel parking lot in front of the Road Hog and killed the engine, but he didn't get out right away. Justin had to be lying. The kid would consider it a good practical joke to get Caleb riled up and have him driving all the way into town to see about Melanie.

Melanie herself was probably in on the joke.

Drunk. That was a good one. Melanie never got

drunk. It took her all night long to sip her way through one or two beers. And that certainly didn't make her drunk.

It was much more likely that Justin got hooked up with a woman and didn't want to drive Melanie home. Melanie wouldn't care, because she and Justin were just friends.

But then, he would have sworn *he* and Melanie were just friends, too, until she'd knocked his socks off with that kiss the other night at the party. Now he wasn't sure what they were to each other.

It flashed through his mind that calling him to come rescue Melanie could be nothing more than a trick to get him to come to Billy Ray's party. Justin and Melanie weren't above such a scheme.

It wasn't that he didn't like Billy Ray. How could you not like a guy who put up with everyone calling him by his first and last names together, all his life? His name wasn't Billy Ray Somebody. Ray was not his middle name, it was his last name. But for some reason, everyone in his family was known by their first and last names joined together. And the names always ran together as if they were one word: BillyRay, his brother DonnieRay, their daddy JuniorRay, their sister ConnieRay, and their mother, Mrs.Ray, pronounced MizRay. MizRay, as far as anyone could tell, did not have a first name other than Miz.

Caleb liked them all just fine. It was only that Billy Ray and his crowd were several years younger than Caleb, and he could take only so much rowdy partying.

Could it be that at thirty-three he was getting old?

Nah, thirty-three wasn't old. Never mind the aching muscles as he finally climbed out of his pickup. Muscles were supposed to ache after a long hard day.

The noise from the band was loud in the parking lot. He took a deep breath and braced himself before pushing the door of the Road Hog open and stepping inside. The blast of sound that hit him made him wince. The wall of smoke choked him. Two more good reasons to have stayed home—preservation of his lungs and eardrums.

"Hey, Caleb!" Billy Ray himself, obviously just coming from the men's room, spotted him instantly and gave Caleb a hearty slap on the back. Or, he would have, if he hadn't been three sheets to the wind. His aim was off and his hand barely glanced off Caleb's shoulder. But the force of his own movement, without Caleb's solid back to stop him, nearly sent him face-first to the floor. He staggered, then righted himself and grinned sloppily. "Glad you came, buddy. Come on over to my table and have a beer."

Caleb tucked his hands into his back pockets and pretended he hadn't heard the invitation. "Looks like a big party." He had to shout to make himself heard over the band and the crowd.

"It's the best!" Billy Ray answered. "Oops. There's Carol Anne flaggin' me down." He wiggled his eyebrows. "Wouldn't wanna keep the lady waiting, now, would I?"

Caleb laughed, as he was meant to. "Not if you're smart, pardner."

"Oh, yeah," Billy Ray said, swaying past Caleb toward the well-endowed redhead waving her arms in the air. "If there's one thing Billy Ray is, it's smart, and don't let anyone tell you different."

Caleb shook his head as Billy Ray plowed his way through the crowd of people. Yep, he would just as soon have stayed home. That didn't make him old, it just, in his book, made him sensible.

Now all he had to do was find Melanie through the smoke and the throng and call Justin's bluff about her being drunk.

This was one of those occasions when being six feet tall came in handy. There were some men taller than he was, but they were either on the dance floor, sitting at a table, or leaning on the bar. Without too much stretching on his part he was able to see pretty much the entire room.

Just then the band ended their number and a two-second lull occurred before the roar of voices resumed over the scattering of applause. Into that two-second lull came a sharp whistle from near the tiny dance floor in front of the band at the opposite end of the room from where Caleb stood.

The whistle was, if one could be, familiar. He glanced over and saw Justin. Caleb nodded that he'd spotted him, and Justin pointed toward the booths along the far wall.

And there sat Melanie in the front corner booth. Maybe *sat* wasn't the right word, as she was more or less slumped into the corner. She looked as if any moment she would simply slide right out of the booth and end up in the floor beneath the table.

Good grief, had Justin been telling the truth? Was she really drunk?

As he worked his way to her side he worried over what could have caused her to get herself in such a state.

He remembered that lost look on her face Saturday night at the party, remembered thinking she was upset over Sloan's marriage to Emily. She had denied it, but now, seeing her drunk, for what might be the first time in her life, he had to wonder.

Saturday night she'd said that whatever was bothering her had nothing to do with Sloan. Caleb knew Melanie pretty well, and he couldn't imagine what could be hurting her enough to have her acting so out of character.

"Hey, there." He slid in across from her, more than surprised that someone as popular and well-liked as Melanie was alone in the booth.

Her eyes were closed. For a minute he was afraid she had fallen asleep. Or passed out, if she was really as soused as Justin said.

"Go away," she said. "There's only enough beer for one, and I'm the one."

The pitcher was full, her glass half so.

"Looks to me," he said, "as if you've had more than your fair share already."

Melanie cracked one eye partially open then groaned. Great. She'd either had way too much to drink, or not nearly enough. She was hallucinating. She had to be, because she knew Caleb wasn't really sitting across from her. No way. She'd made sure to find out that he was not coming to…to… Oh, yeah. Billy Ray's birthday party. The Road Hog. That's where she was.

But Caleb wasn't there. She'd ridden to town with Justin. Not Caleb.

"I definitely need another beer." She raised her glass, but the apparition across from her reached out and snatched it from her hand. "Hey!"

"No more for you, pal."

Melanie frowned and squinted to see more clearly. "Lips?"

The apparition frowned back. "What about them?"

"''Zat you?''

''Jeez, how drunk are you? It's me, Caleb. Are you ready to go home?''

She hiccuped, then giggled. ''I think I'm too drive to drunk.''

He muttered something that sounded like, ''The understatement of the year.''

''Hey, I resemble that statement.''

Caleb laughed and shook his head. He'd never seen her like this. ''You certainly do. Come on, woman, let's get you out of here.''

She poked out her lower lip in a stupendous pout. ''Don't wanna go home.''

Caleb slid out of the booth. He stepped to her side of the table and reached for her arm, intrigued by the strength he felt there. He shouldn't let her strength surprise him; he knew she worked probably as hard as he did. He decided he liked that firm muscle beneath his hand.

''Come on,'' he said. ''We'll go someplace else, then.'' He wasn't, as a rule, a liar, but just then he would have promised her anything to get her to get up and walk out the door with him. He hoped to God she could still walk. If he had to carry her through this crowd of her friends she would never live it down. Which meant she would never forgive him.

But she let him tug her across the seat to stand beside him. She wobbled a little but stayed upright.

Caleb wrapped his arm around her waist and started her toward the door. She leaned against him and stumbled over her own feet.

''Oops.'' She giggled.

''You're going to love hearing about this tomorrow,'' he muttered.

She flung her head back to look up at him and nearly threw them both over backward. "What?" she yelled. "Where are we going?"

"Out of here."

They made it out the door without much trouble. Most of the crowd didn't notice they were leaving, so only a few yelled out to say good-night. The gravel in the parking lot made for tricky footing for Melanie. He would have simply picked her up and carried her—she wasn't in much condition to object—but there were several people around and he didn't want to have to deal with the talk such a move would surely generate. He took most of Melanie's weight against his hip. All she had to do was move her feet, and finally they made it to his truck, where he belted her into the passenger seat.

"Where we goin'?" she asked, swaying as he turned right out of the parking lot.

"You already asked that."

"I did?" *Hic. Giggle.*

"Jeez, you are snockered." He glanced over in time to see her blink once, slowly. She reminded him of a baby owl.

"How 'bout that. I guess I am. Snockered."

"I'm wondering why that is," Caleb said.

Hic. Giggle. "'Cuz I drank too much beer." She gave an emphatic nod. The movement would have overbalanced her and sent her tumbling to the floor-board had it not been for the seat and shoulder belts.

"Easy, there." Caleb reached over and pulled her back upright. Her head fell against the headrest and stayed there. He would have wished that she would just go ahead and pass out, except then he would have to get her into her house, and he didn't particularly want to have to explain to Ralph why he was bringing his pride and joy home drunk as the proverbial skunk.

And if the worst should happen and Ralph wasn't home, Caleb would have to put her to bed.

"Don't you dare fall asleep," he ordered sharply.

"Sleep, sleep, sleep. Don' wanna sleep. Where we goin'? I wanna dance."

Caleb turned on the radio to a country station. "Knock yourself out. Figuratively speaking."

"Knock myself out." She gave herself a mock punch to the head. "Pow." She laughed so hard she fell against the door.

Caleb winced. She was strapped in, but that didn't mean he wanted that door to fly open. Leaning as far as he could, he reached behind her head and pushed the door lock on her door.

"Oh, oh! I love this song." She leaped toward the radio. It took her three tries, but she finally managed to turn up the volume and sing along.

Since Caleb had spent most of the past two days reliving that kiss they'd shared on the makeshift dance floor Saturday night, he wished heartily that she had picked some song other than the old Conway Twitty hit about wanting a lover with a slow hand. Caleb did not need the pictures that took over his mind.

Retracing a trip he'd made at least a hundred times in his life, Caleb slowed and turned off the highway onto the Pruitt Ranch driveway. But for his headlights it was pitch-black out here. He had to take it even slower than he had when he brought her home the day before, because he couldn't see where the next pothole might be.

Potholes obviously were no concern for Melanie.

She sat next to him singing at the top of her lungs. Currently it was a commercial jingle about car mufflers.

"We're here," he said unnecessarily.

"No, no, no." She groaned. "I tol' you I di'n wanna come home."

"Yeah, you told me." He parked next to the back door. The house was dark, and the yard and driveway, lit by the utility light next to the house, showed her lone vehicle. After ten on a weeknight and her dad wasn't home.

"Not my business," he muttered as he got out and went around to haul Melanie out.

She did not cooperate. Part of that was on purpose, because she really didn't want to go into the house, and she kept saying so as she held on to the truck door when he urged her out of her seat. But part of her lack of cooperation was because she was too snockered to stand up straight.

"Okay." He slipped one arm around her waist and lifted her weight onto his hip again. It had worked well enough at the parking lot. "Here we go."

At the back door he pulled open the storm door and tried the knob. It was locked. No surprise there.

"Where's your key?" he asked.

She blinked up at him, doing that little owl thing again, and giggled. "You're so cute. Did I ever tell you how cute you are?"

"Come on, you're not that drunk. Your key, Melanie. Where's your house key?"

She gave him a sly smile. "My pocket."

"Well, get it so I can get you inside."

"No."

Caleb dropped his forehead to rest against hers and

sighed. "Come on, Mel, be a sport. Give me your key."

"You have to kiss me first."

Caleb jerked his head up. In the glow of the utility light he stared at her, stunned. "I take it back. You're drunker than I thought. Give me your key."

Her bottom lip poked out. "You're not gonna kiss me?"

"We did that the other night, remember? I got the impression you wished we hadn't. Now be a pal and give me your key."

"I know you liked kissing me."

"Sugarpie, a dead man would like kissing you." *Please, God, let her be too drunk to remember I said that.* "Now give me your key."

That sly smile she gave him a moment ago returned. "Why don't you get it yourself?"

Sweat popped out along his upper lip. He could almost feel his hand pushing into her pocket, feeling the shape of her beneath a single layer of fabric.

He braced his hands on her shoulders. "If I have to get it myself I'm going to hold you upside down by your ankles and shake you until the key falls out."

Now her pout came back. "You're no fun." She jammed her right hand into her front pocket and pulled out a key. And promptly dropped it. "Oops." *Giggle. Hic.*

Caleb spent the next several minutes on his hands and knees, in the semidark, swearing, until he finally found the key on the edge of the bottom step.

"Eureka!" Melanie cried with a wave of her arms that nearly sent her tumbling off the steps.

"Whoa, there." Caleb caught her by the arm and steadied her. While he unlocked the door, she moaned.

"Caleb?"

"Here we go." He pushed open the door and reached inside and turned on the kitchen light.

She swayed against him. "Caleb, is this room s'pose to be spinning?"

"Oh no you don't." He swept her into the room and closed the door. "Don't you dare pass out or get sick on me."

She leaned against him. "I think I need to…"

"I hope you're going to say lie down." He helped her across the kitchen and down the hall. Caleb got her through her bedroom door and lowered her to sit on the side of the bed.

She fell back, her arms spread wide. "Ahhh."

Caleb turned on the bedside lamp. "You're not sick?"

"Nope. I'm fine, fine, fine." She looked at him and wiggled her eyebrows. "You're lookin' pretty fine yourself, Lips."

"I'll ignore that. Let's get these boots off." He straightened her on the bed, then tugged off her boots, leaving her thick white socks on. "Better?"

"Mmm." She flexed her toes. "Oh, yeah." She tugged her shirttail free and unbuckled her belt.

Caleb swallowed. "What are you doing?"

"Getting comfor—" She unzipped her jeans. "Comorb—" With a wiggle of her hips she started tugging the denim down her hips. "Comftorble."

He stood beside the bed, helpless to stop her, helpless to look away. Had her legs always been that long, that perfect?

With a final kick of her feet the jeans did a neat little soar-and-dive and fell into a puddle on the floor.

Caleb couldn't look anymore. He reached across her

and tugged the comforter until it covered her from the waist down. Feeling much better, and not a little proud of himself, he propped his hands on his hips and wished he knew why she'd felt the need to drink the way she had tonight. "Need anything else?"

"Uh-huh."

"What?"

She crooked a finger at him. "Come here."

He stepped closer. "What do you need?"

"Come cos— Closer. Come closer."

"I'm right here, Mel."

She wiggled sideways on the bed, then patted the space beside her hip. "Here."

Caleb sat on the edge of the bed and leaned toward her. "What is it? Are you sick?"

"No." She shook her head, then closed her eyes and moaned. "Oh, I shouldn't have done that. Remind me not to move my head again."

"Don't move your head again."

"Gee, thanks."

"You're welcome. You want to tell me why you did this to yourself?"

"You wanna kiss me again?"

If she had needed to get his attention, she sure did it. "What?" he asked, certain that he did not want her to repeat the question.

"You liked kissing me."

"Melanie…"

She reached up and traced a finger across his mouth. "You've got great lips."

Caleb jerked his head back. Letting her touch his lips was not a good idea. Not when he wanted— badly—to taste hers. "Three pitchers of beer, huh?"

She slipped her hands around his neck and locked her fingers together. "And your point is?"

"Come on, Mel, let go."

"Not until you tell me."

"Tell you what?"

She licked her lips. "Tell me you liked kissing me."

Lamplight glistened along her moist mouth, making him want to groan. Instead, he swallowed. "I liked kissing you."

"Then do it again." She tugged him closer.

"And have you accuse me tomorrow that I took advantage of you?"

A giggle escaped her. "Oh, goody. You're going to take advantage of me?"

"I am not." He pulled her hands from behind his neck, but she then slid them around his chest. "Come on, quit fooling around."

"Well, that's typical. All I wanted was a kiss, and you want to fool around."

"If you weren't three sheets to the wind I might just give you what you think you want."

"Promises, promises. Come here." She tugged sharply, throwing him off balance. He caught himself on his forearms before crushing her beneath his weight. "You don't have to take advantage of me. I'll take advantage of you."

"Melanie."

"Caleb. I've never known you to talk so much. Are you scared of me?"

Somewhere in the back of his mind he realized that she wasn't slurring her words quite as much as she had been, but the thought disappeared, along with his common sense, when he admitted, "Terrified."

But really, he thought, gazing into her eyes and on

down that pert nose to those soft lips. What would it hurt if he kissed her? She wanted him to. And in the morning she probably wouldn't even remember it.

And that was disgusting. She didn't know what she was doing. He had never taken advantage of a woman in his life. He wasn't about to start with a trusted friend. This was Melanie, for crying out loud. She trusted him. He couldn't betray that trust.

"I'll be gentle," she whispered.

"Melanie."

"Are you going to make me beg?"

All the strength went out of his knees, his arms. He lowered toward her until there was nothing but a scant breath separating his mouth from hers. Then there was nothing at all, because he was unable to stop himself from taking what she offered. Giving what she asked for.

Her taste was hot and sweet, with a hint of beer that made him smile against her mouth.

When she traced his lower lip with her tongue, he forgot all about smiling. He forgot he shouldn't be kissing his friend. He forgot that she probably didn't know what she was doing. He forgot his own name. It didn't matter. He didn't care what his name was—he knew hers. It was Melanie. Sweet, sweet Melanie, who could be as soft as an angel one minute, sharp as a blade the next, and just now, in his arms—how had his arms come to be around her?—as fiery and lethal as a bolt of lightning.

Then suddenly her mouth went slack, her arms slid from around his back to fall to her sides on the bed.

Caleb raised his head and looked at her. "Melanie?"

Her eyes were closed. She had passed out.

It was a sign, Caleb thought as he pushed himself up and off of her.

Damn. He didn't even remember crawling on top of her. Another few minutes and he might have done something they would both be a lot sorrier for than a simple kiss or two.

Not that kissing Melanie even began to resemble simple. They had too much history between then, as neighbors, as friends, for them to change the status quo without some careful consideration.

He looked down at her sweet, familiar face, her sable-brown hair spread out messily across the pillow. He was halfway toward touching that hair when he stopped himself and backed away. He had no business touching her while she slept. No business standing over her, watching her.

He turned off the lamp and left the room. As he stepped into the hall, a delicate snore followed him. He smiled.

Chapter Three

The sofa in the Pruitts' living room was almost long enough to allow Caleb to stretch out. Almost, but not quite. During the night, he was certain he'd set a new record for tossing and turning, if anyone kept track of things like that. Now the sun was coming up, yet he felt as if he hadn't slept a wink.

Of course, sleep might have come easier if he hadn't kept seeing Melanie's long, bare legs, and the lower edge of her white lace panties every time he closed his eyes.

Her father hadn't returned, and Caleb hadn't been able to go home and leave her alone last night. The girl he'd known since childhood, the woman she had grown into, would not have gotten drunk last night, or any night, without a damn good reason. It wasn't like her.

Maybe he'd been right Saturday night. Maybe she

really wasn't over Sloan. Caleb couldn't think of anything else that would bother her so much, and he knew her well. But a broken heart? Yeah, that would do it for Melanie. She might act tough as nails, could be as hard and mean as she had to be when the situation warranted, but she had the most tender heart on the planet.

When he crawled from the sofa it took him a minute to straighten up. He should have slept on the floor. It might have been harder, but at least it wouldn't have been too short.

He went to Melanie's door and found her sound asleep, sprawled on her back, her hands over her head as if in surrender. No way was he waking her.

He checked again to see if her father had returned, but there was still no sign of Ralph Pruitt. On a ranch at six-thirty on a Tuesday morning there was always work to be done. Where the hell was the man?

Caleb went to the kitchen and started a pot of coffee. While it brewed he stepped out the back door to have a look around. The air was cool and damp, the wind light. From the chicken house across the driveway came a noisy fuss and clatter, hens bickering amongst each other, a couple of roosters crowing for all they were worth.

Not knowing if the Pruitts let their chickens out during the day or kept them penned and safe from predators, Caleb decided to leave the birds alone and headed for the barn instead.

There he found three pretty mares pacing restlessly in their stalls.

"Good morning, ladies. I bet you'd like to get out of there. How about a handful of oats first? Maybe a little grooming?"

* * *

Melanie came awake in slow, painful stages. Then wished she hadn't. Her head! How had a hammer ended up inside her head, and who the devil was banging it against the inside of her skull?

"Somebody shoot me, please," she moaned. The beer. Why, why, why had she drank so much beer? For that matter, *how* had she drunk that much? She'd never been able to hold that much water in one evening, let alone beer.

Too bad she hadn't gotten even drunker. Maybe then she wouldn't be remembering... Good grief! What had she done? Caleb brought her home and had been sweet enough to take care of her, tuck her in, and she had...she had... She'd done something, she knew she had. It involved mouths and lips and tongues, but it was all fuzzy in her pain-fogged brain.

In sheer misery she rolled to her side. The light from the window blinded her.

Light? Good grief! If it was that light, it was late. She'd slept half the morning away.

The mares! Oh, those poor babies.

Melanie tossed the comforter aside and pushed herself up. Every muscle and joint screamed in protest, and her stomach heaved. She wrapped her arms around her gut and moaned.

"I will not throw up. I will not throw up. I will not throw up."

She waited, breathing deeply, to be sure the mantra was going to work. When everything stayed settled, she slid off the side of the bed and tested the strength of her legs. Since they seemed to work, she staggered from the bedroom toward the back door.

Coffee. The aroma reached out and tempted her to

pause for a cup of sustenance, but she feared that if she gave in, it might be an hour before she was able to force herself outside, and the mares were surely impatient by now, wondering what had happened to her. Much longer and they'd be kicking down their stalls.

She steeled herself against the seductive smell of coffee and opened the back door. Only then, as the rush of cool air made goose bumps rise on her legs, did she look down at herself. She was wearing last night's shirt and bra, panties, socks, and not a damn thing more.

To heck with it. She jammed her feet into the extra pair of boots she kept by the door and slammed outside. It was cool but not cold, and there was no one around to see her.

At the sound of the door slamming, the chickens set up a clatter in their fenced pen surrounding the chicken house.

"Yeah, yeah," Melanie called. "I'm coming, babies." It had long been accepted on the PR, although reluctantly by most, that their chickens were for egg production, not for the frying pan. At the age of six, when Melanie caught her mother wringing the neck of a hen that had stopped laying, Melanie had cried for three days and refused to eat. She most especially had refused to eat Esmeralda, her favorite pretty bird.

Her parents had tried and tried to explain the realities of ranch life, of where food came from, but Melanie hadn't budged. She could eat beef. The ranch produced so many steers each year, and they kept them for only a few months, out in the pastures. She never really had much of a chance to get attached to any of them.

The chickens were a different story. There were a scant dozen of them, and they were right there by the house all the time, and her parents had never warned her not to get attached, not to name them, not to pet the tamer ones.

Eat them? No way!

Of course, her attitude made her the butt of many a joke among her friends, but she didn't care. To her, eating one of her own chickens would be like eating the family dog. She could eat the Colonel's chicken, or the grocery store's, without a qualm. But not her own.

She entered the chicken yard, leaving the gate open as she scattered grain on the ground. The birds would wander in and out through the day, but they wouldn't go far; the hens were attached to their nest boxes and the scratch Melanie fed them every day.

The mares were waiting, so Melanie didn't linger. Her boots scuffed a fast trail across the gravel and dirt to the barn. It was only as she neared that it dawned on her that the barn door was open. She was positive she had closed it before leaving with Justin the evening before. She would not have been so careless as to have left it open.

Hearing what sounded like a voice coming from inside the barn, Melanie darted to the side of the big door. Steam bubbled inside her, along with a small dash of fear. If one of those goons her father owed money to had come to the PR again as they had a few months earlier to demand she pay her father's debt, there would be hell to pay.

Hearing another low murmur, Melanie slipped through the door and into the deep shadows of the first stall, which was open and empty. For once she was glad her father had taken to leaving tools there instead of putting them away where they belonged. She would have preferred a pitchfork, but the shovel in the corner would do just as well. Quietly she picked it up and peered down the center of the barn.

A man stood at one of the mare's stalls, his back toward Melanie.

Melanie gritted her teeth and gripped the shovel tightly in both hands. No stranger snuck in and messed around in her barn, by damn. She crept soundlessly across the dirt floor of the barn. The creep never heard her coming. She hefted the shovel in the air, and when she knew she was close enough, she swung.

She would never know if she made a sound, or if some sixth sense alerted him to her presence. Either way, just as she swung, he stood and turned.

Caleb!

With a shout of protest he raised an arm to fend off the blow.

Melanie tried to halt her swing, but it was too late. She did manage to shift her aim, thank God. The steel spade whacked him solidly on the shoulder rather than the head, where she had originally aimed. Still, the ring of the connecting blow echoed through the barn. As did Caleb's brief grunt of pain.

"Oh no!" Melanie cried.

"Damnation, woman, what the hell was that for?"

"Caleb, I'm sorry. I thought— I'm so sorry. Did I hurt you?"

He grimaced and rubbed his shoulder. "What do you think? You whacked me a good one."

Now that she realized he wasn't seriously hurt, Melanie was disgusted with herself. She must be more hungover than she'd thought not to have noticed Caleb's pickup, which, now that she thought about it, was parked outside the back door of the house. Idiot that she was, she had walked right past it without paying attention.

Even without noticing his pickup, she should have recognized, even from the back, a man she had known her entire life. Should have recognized a voice nearly as familiar to her as her own.

"What I want to know," Caleb went on, "is why?"

"Never mind." She tossed the shovel aside and took him by the arm. "Let's get some ice on that shoulder."

"I'm all right." He pulled free of her. "Let's get the mares taken care of first."

Melanie was torn. Taking care of Caleb was a need. The mares were a responsibility. Caleb was right. The mares came first.

It took mere minutes to see to the mares and turn them out into the pasture for the day, then she was back at Caleb's side, leading him toward the house. She took him into the kitchen and pushed him down onto a chair at the table.

"Take off your shirt," Melanie said as she turned away and opened the freezer.

"All you had to do was ask," Caleb said. "You didn't have to hit me with a shovel first."

"Very funny." She pulled out a clear, zippered plastic bag of corn kernels. She had grown the corn, sliced the kernels from the ears herself and had the nicks in her knuckles to prove it. She turned back toward Caleb, but stopped where she stood.

She had seen him without a shirt before, many times, she was sure, but she didn't remember the sight of his bare chest ever causing this hitch in her breathing before, or this sudden need to swallow. To touch. To feel.

The hangover must be having an even stranger effect on her than she'd realized. With a shake of her head she carried the frozen corn to him and gently placed it over the red spot on his shoulder.

"You're not going to kiss it first?"

Melanie narrowed her eyes at him. "You're sure full of yourself this morning. What are you still doing here, anyway? You look like you slept in that shirt."

"I could say the same, but at least I'm wearing jeans. Not that I'm complaining about your clothes, or lack thereof. Actually, I kinda like this look on you."

Dumbfounded, Melanie looked down at her bare legs. "Oh." In her book, there was nothing that looked more ridiculous than the combination of cowboy boots and bare legs. With her socks showing out the tops of the boots, no less. "Ugh."

Then she glanced up at Caleb and realized he was not looking at her boots with the socks showing above them. His gaze rested somewhat higher, namely the end of her shirttail, which was almost embarrassingly high on her thighs. "Pervert." She reached out and pinched his uninjured shoulder.

"Hey, what was that for?" He rubbed the new red spot. "Got another bag of corn?" he grumbled.

"Baby." She tried to step away, but he put a hand on her hip. She stopped instantly. His touch, through the cotton of her shirt, was warm, and felt much more intimate than it should.

"You didn't think I was such a baby last night," he said quietly, his gaze capturing hers and holding it like a magnet.

Melanie's pulse jumped. "I...don't remember much... about last night."

Leaving his hand on her hip, Caleb tossed the bag of corn onto the table and rose from the chair to stand before her. Close before her. "One of the things I've always admired about you was that you've always known, and admitted, that you're a lousy liar.''

Heat stung her cheeks. She didn't need a mirror to tell her they were as red as a Hereford's hind end. ''Yeah, well, it was worth a try.''

With his fingers he smoothed a strand of hair from her face. It was all she could do to keep from leaning into his touch. What was the matter with her?

''Do you want to talk about it?''

''You're kidding, right? Talk about how I got drunk and embarrassed myself last night?''

''Why did you get drunk? It's not like you.''

Melanie shrugged. ''I don't know. I guess I was just more stupid than usual.''

He placed a finger beneath her chin and tilted her face up toward his. ''You are not, nor have you ever been, stupid.''

She forced a wry grin. ''I was last night.''

''I hope you mean because you drank too much, not because you kissed me.''

''Oh, please.'' She rolled her eyes. ''Don't remind me.''

''Maybe I want to remind you.''

Melanie knew, from the look in his eyes and the tone in his voice, that he was not talking about reminding her of drinking too much. She swallowed. ''Why?''

''Aren't you even a little curious to see where this might lead us?''

''No.'' She shook her head hard. ''We don't need to be led anywhere. We do great without kissing.''

''Yeah.'' He pulled her close and rested his cheek against the top of her head. His arms slipped around her and held her loosely. ''You're right. We've always done great, you and me.''

They had stood this way so many times before, Melanie thought. A hundred, a thousand times or more, but never quite like this. There was comfort, as there always had been. Whenever she needed holding to ease an ache inside, Caleb was always there with his broad chest and steady heart. And there was strength, as always, in his muscled arms.

But today there was more. There was a tension, a new anticipation that hummed between them because now they knew what could happen if their lips met. Melanie both feared and reveled in the warring emotions. Both feared and reveled in the feel of his bare chest beneath her splayed fingers. Without any conscious command or permission from her brain, her fingers flexed. Caressed. Beneath them Caleb's muscles jerked.

"Sorry," she murmured.

Maybe he should be, too, Caleb thought, but he wasn't. He wanted her to do it again. He liked feeling her hands on his flesh. It seemed impossible. She was his friend. They had touched each other, casually, a zillion times over the years. Not once, in his memory, had her touch made his pulse spike this way.

Yes, he wanted her to touch him again.

He raised his head and looked down into her emerald-green eyes. If they moved their feet they'd be dancing.

"What are we doing, Caleb?"

"Are we supposed to know?"

"Shouldn't we?"

"Maybe." He brushed his nose along the length of hers. "Or maybe we should just…" He brushed his lips across hers.

Her lips parted on a quick intake of breath. Caleb

dived in, and it happened again, that sharp tingling along his spine. That zap of lightning, the clichéd fireworks exploding in his head.

Melanie felt it, too, that startling awareness, the sheer intensity of which stole her breath and pulled a moan from her throat. Her nerves danced, her blood heated. She pressed herself closer to Caleb's lean, hard body, craving a closer, more intimate connection.

He obliged her, his hands sliding down to cup her hips and pull her flush against him, giving her proof that her blood wasn't all that was heated between them.

Another moan tore from her throat. She arched against him, reveling in the feel of his erection and of her nipples hardening in response. She dragged her hands down his chest, around his waist, across his back. His skin was hot and smooth and sleek, with firm muscles beneath that spoke of steely strength.

The need for breath broke them apart. The need for sanity pushed them each back a step, made them look away from each other, he over her head, she at his shoulder.

Melanie struggled for something to say, some way to explain away what had just happened. Barring that, something to distract them both. Then it came, like a gift, wafting across the room.

"Coffee," she blurted. "I need coffee."

When she spun away toward the coffeemaker, Caleb took in a deep breath and let it out. She obviously didn't want to talk about it. And really, he thought, what was there to say? The whole situation was crazy. Best friends weren't supposed to set off fireworks when they kissed. Hell, they weren't supposed to be kissing, not like that, in the first place.

But damned if he didn't want to do it again, and

again, and see where it led them. For now, however, it might be wiser to change the subject.

"So where is everybody?" He'd been wondering that since before he'd crawled off the sofa earlier. If she wouldn't talk about the two of them and whatever this kissing thing was that was going on with them, maybe he could get her to talk about something else. "I didn't see your men when I was out earlier."

She shrugged. "Day off."

Caleb eyed her skeptically. "Tuesday is their day off?"

She poured two mugs of coffee and handed him one without speaking.

"How about your dad? Is it his day off, too?"

"Lord only knows where he is, because I sure don't."

The sharp bitterness in her voice surprised him. "How long's he been gone?"

"What, are you writing a book? You're sure nosy all of a sudden. Maybe you think a couple of kisses gives you the right to give me the third degree, but if that's what you're thinking, buster, you can just think again."

Caleb stared, astounded. "Whoa, there. What brought that on?"

She whirled away so fast that coffee sloshed from her mug to splatter on the floor.

Caleb set his mug, along with his bag of frozen corn, on the table. At the counter next to the sink he tore a paper towel from the roll mounted beneath the upper cabinet and wiped up the spill on the floor. He threw the wadded towel into the trash, then turned to face Melanie.

"We've already established that you're a lousy liar,

so why don't you just tell me what's going on around here? How long has your dad been gone? Has something happened to him? Where are your men? And why is this place starting to look like nobody's been here for weeks?''

Her cheeks turned bright red. She moved to step around him.

"Melanie, I'm not trying to embarrass you or stick my nose into your business. I'm trying to find out what kind of trouble my best friend and neighbor is in so I can figure out how to help. The more you refuse to answer, the worse I'm going to think it is. Now just tell me, dammit. Where's your dad?''

What did it matter, Melanie thought, if she told him the truth? If she couldn't tell somebody soon, the whole ugly mess was liable to explode in her from the inside out. All her life, whenever she had trouble, Caleb was the one she had always taken it to. He had never made her feel small or stupid, had never betrayed a confidence. He had always listened, and, if asked, offered sound advice.

But, oh, how she did not want to have this discussion. It was embarrassing. Humiliating.

"I don't know," she blurted. "I don't know where Daddy is, and right now I don't much care.''

"That's a hell of a thing to say. What do you mean you don't know where he is? He didn't come home last night.''

"I know that. He's off gambling somewhere. Again.''

"Ah, hell, Melanie, I'm sorry. What happened?'' he asked quietly. "I thought he was doing good, going to those Gamblers Anonymous meetings up in the city.''

She shook her head and plunked her mug down on the counter next to the sink. "He was. He was doing fine until he decided he didn't need the meetings anymore and stopped going. Within a week he started draining cash out of the ranch.''

"Ah, damn, Melanie, I'm sorry. How bad is it? Do you need help?''

She gave a short, harsh laugh. "Help? I had to let the men go three weeks ago. Daddy thinks I'm blowing things out of proportion, but he hasn't seen anything yet.''

"What do you mean?''

"When he needs cash he uses his ATM card. Yesterday I canceled it. I also canceled the credit card Mama's been playing with.''

"Did you do that yesterday, too?''

She nodded and took a sip of her coffee. "Yeah. And I think Mama's sick but I can't reach her to find out.''

"What makes you think that?''

"There was a big charge on the credit card from a clinic.''

All of that to handle, and then, he thought, she'd gone out and gotten drunk.

"I'm hungry," she said suddenly. "How about breakfast?''

"You cooking?''

She laughed. "As if you would. As if you could.''

"Hey, do you think Grandmother raised the three of us to be helpless? I can scramble eggs with the best of them.''

"Well, well. Imagine learning something new about you after all these years. You're in charge of the eggs.''

Breakfast turned into the most awkward affair either of them could remember experiencing. The kitchen was not small, yet it seemed every time one of them turned around, the other was there, too close. By the time the meal was on the table they were practically tiptoeing around each other.

The meal itself wasn't much better, except they didn't have to worry about bumping into each other. Except with their gazes, which were quickly averted.

They used to enjoy each other's company. They used to be able to laugh and talk about anything or nothing. Now it seemed they couldn't even look at each other.

Melanie couldn't stand it. She wanted her friend back. She laid down her fork with a definite clatter and glared across the table at Caleb.

"Is this how it's going to be between us?" she asked. "Have we ruined our friendship?"

"Come on, don't say that."

"Well, look at us," she cried. "This is—this is the pits is what it is."

"If you think I'm sorry, I'm not. I'm sorry you feel awkward, but what happened between us was something special, and you know it. I won't apologize for it, and if you say you regret it you're a liar, and we've already established you're no good at that. You've never been a liar before. Don't start now. Besides," he added with a narrowing of his eyes and a quirk of his lips. "You started it."

"Oh, well." She threw a hand in the air. "That helps. *You started it,*" she mimicked. "How intelligent. How mature. Am I supposed to come back with *Did not* so you can tack on a *did too* for good measure? Then we can stick our tongues out at each other like two adults."

"Now there's a picture," Caleb said. "But if you're

going to stick your tongue out, you should come over here and do it up close.''

"Don't be a jerk, Caleb.''

"Then don't be an idiot,'' he countered. "We kissed. It was terrific. We did it again, twice, and it was just as terrific. Why should that ruin our friendship?''

Melanie groaned in frustration. "If I wasn't so hungover I'm sure I'd have a coherent answer to that. Meanwhile I'll be your friend and tell you to put that ice back on your shoulder.''

He grimaced and reached for the bag of corn. "If you were my friend you wouldn't have clobbered me in the first place. Care to explain that, pal?''

She scrunched up her face. "I did say I was sorry, didn't I?''

"You did. So do you always swing a shovel when you find a man in your barn?''

"Damn right I do. I thought you were another one of those creeps coming to collect on one of Daddy's debts.''

Caleb's heart gave a hard thump. "What? Are you saying you've got thumb breakers coming around here hitting you up because of your dad?''

She shrugged and looked away, a flush of embarrassment coloring her cheeks.

Damn, Caleb thought. Things were worse, much worse at the PR than he could have imagined. With their hired hands gone, Ralph off God knew where, Melanie was left alone to deal not only with the work of running the ranch, but the fallout from Ralph's gambling.

The situation, as far as Caleb was concerned, was intolerable. "When's your dad due back?''

"I have no idea."

Caleb thought a minute, then nodded. "All right, then." He got up and went to the wall phone beside the back door and called home. Sloan's wife, Emily, answered.

"Hey, it's me. I need a favor."

"Caleb, where are you? We've been worried to death."

"Sorry," he said, realizing he should have called home last night. "I gave Melanie a ride home last night. She didn't feel good—"

Behind him Melanie snorted, sounding like a disgruntled hog.

"—and her dad wasn't home, so I stayed."

"Is she all right? What do you need me to do?"

"She's fine. It looks like Ralph's going to be gone for a few days, so I'm going to stay over here and give Melanie a hand."

"Caleb, no," Melanie protested.

Caleb ignored her and spoke to Emily. "Can you gather up enough clean clothes to last me two or three days and have Hector run them over here when he gets a chance?"

Emily readily agreed, promising the clean clothes within the hour.

"Caleb," Melanie said after he hung up. "You can't be serious about staying here."

"Sure I can. That's what friends do, Mel."

"But it's not necessary. You think I can't do my own chores?"

"I think you can do your own chores just fine. But there's no reason you should have to do all of your work, your father's, the work of two hired men, and fight off thumb breakers, all by yourself. And that has nothing," he added to forestall the argument he could see forming in her eyes, "to do with your being a woman."

"I wasn't going to say that."

He knew better. Knew her better. "What is it with you today?" he demanded. "That's at least the third time you've lied to me."

"That wasn't a lie," she protested. "It was a denial."

Caleb rolled his eyes.

"In any case, you're not staying here."

"Yes," he said emphatically, "I am." He had to. There was a need. If the need was his more than hers, that didn't scare him. Not too much.

The hell it didn't, he thought. He'd known her all his life, but suddenly he felt drawn to her, had a need to be near her that had nothing to do with friendship.

But all that aside, he couldn't leave her here alone to fend for herself, especially if there was the chance of some goon showing up to make mischief.

He'd like to punch Ralph Pruitt square in the nose.

"Caleb, I appreciate the offer, but I neither want nor need your pity."

"That's a stupid thing to say, and it's mean. Since when have I ever pitied you?"

Melanie snapped her teeth together. The truth was, he had pitied her plenty of times over the years, whenever she had cried on his shoulder because Sloan wouldn't pay her any attention. She had deserved Caleb's pity then because she had been pretty damn pitiful.

"I'm not staying because I feel sorry for you," he claimed, and she believed him. "I'm staying because I'd do the same for any neighbor, so I can't really see myself doing any less for a neighbor who happens to be my closest damn friend, all right? I don't care if you need me here or not. I need to be here. Get over it.''

Melanie threw her hands in the air. "I'm going to take a shower. Toss that bag of corn back in the freezer before it thaws and trade it for the peas.''

Caleb couldn't help smirking. "Yes, ma'am.''

With a snarl of irritation, she spun on her heel and stomped from the room in bare legs and cowboy boots.

For his sake, Caleb hoped that when she came back she'd have on some damn pants. Platonic friends weren't supposed to have legs that long and shapely.

When Melanie returned to the kitchen thirty minutes later she did indeed have on some damn pants. Jeans, faded, worn and soft-looking. Her dark hair was still wet and slicked back from a face scrubbed clean. Her eyes, while still a shade on the bloodshot side, were nonetheless alert, even as they avoided his gaze.

She stood in the middle of the room and blinked. "You cleaned the kitchen?''

He frowned. "Yeah, so?''

"So? You guys over at the Cherokee Rose have a housekeeper who I happen to know cleans up after all of you and keeps your house spotless so you don't have to lift a finger in that area.''

"That she does.'' He gave the counter a final swipe with the dishrag in his hand. "But Earline's only been with us a few years. If you think Grandmother didn't make the three of us clean up after ourselves—''

"Got it. And you're right. I know she raised the three of you, and she wouldn't have waited on you hand and foot or cleaned that big house all by herself. Not Rose.''

"You got that right."

"That's what makes her one of my heroes."

Outside, a pickup pulled up. Melanie folded her arms and watched out the window as Caleb went out and took a duffel bag from the young Mexican man behind the wheel.

It was so like Caleb, to see a friend in need and refuse to do anything other than help. This particular friend, however—namely, herself—would breathe a little easier if Caleb went home, but it didn't look as if that was going to happen anytime soon.

A gleam came into her eyes. Maybe she couldn't convince him to go home. So, if he was going to stay, she was going to take full advantage of it and see that some long-postponed work got done around this place. If he thought he was going to get to sit around the house and watch ESPN all day while sipping iced tea, he had another think coming.

She was being ridiculous, she knew. She'd never known Caleb to sit still when there was work to be done, and he was the one who kept pointing out how much work needed to be done on the PR. So she would accept his help.

"That was fast," she said when the pickup drove away and Caleb came back inside.

"Emily's a godsend, and Hector drives fast."

"Hector, huh? A new hand?"

"We took him on a couple of weeks ago."

"Hmm."

"What's that supposed to mean?"

"Nothing." She shrugged. "It's just that there's been a flood of illegal aliens around here lately. Is he local?"

"I don't believe you said that." Caleb gaped at her.

"What?"

"I'd wager that a quarter of this county is of Mexican descent, or Indian." Namely him and his family, part Cherokee, one and all. "Or both. Since when did that matter to you?"

Melanie blinked. "You think I care that he's got dark skin? I can't believe *you* said *that.*"

Caleb turned away and ran his fingers through his hair. He knew better. He knew she wasn't prejudiced. Or, he thought he'd known. She had never seemed to care that his skin was so much darker than hers. And he knew she had friends from school who were Mexican Americans.

"Then what did you mean about Hector?"

"I just meant he didn't look familiar."

"That's not what you meant. Just because you don't recognize him doesn't mean he's an illegal. That's not a logical assumption, even for you."

"What do you mean, even for me?"

"Don't change the subject. What have you got against Mexicans?"

"Nothing," she cried, throwing her hands in the air. "Okay, look. There's a rumor going around that somebody around here is helping illegal aliens hide from Immigration."

"And you think it's us?"

"I'm hoping it's not."

Interesting, Caleb thought. Crazy, but interesting that she would think such a thing. "Would you care?" he asked.

"Of course I would care," she cried. "You think I want to see you and your family get in trouble? Hiding illegal aliens is against the law. Besides which," she added with a quirk of her lips, "I'd think a Native

American would be the last person who'd want to see more foreigners flooding into this country.''

"Hey, I'm only half Indian. Half of my ancestors came over on the *Mayflower*.''

"Yeah, yeah, and the other half met the boat. I've heard that one before. About a hundred times.''

"So all this smoke about Hector and illegal aliens is because you're worried about me?''

"Oh, just go soak your head in the shower.''

"Thanks.'' He hefted his duffel bag. "I was hoping you'd say that.''

While Caleb was in the shower Melanie decided to head out to the barn and get started on what was shaping up to be a long day. She was halfway to the barn when her father sped up the driveway, a giant rooster tail of dust shooting up behind him. He came to a skidding halt a few feet away from Caleb's pickup, got out and slammed the door. He eyed Caleb's rig briefly, shot her a look and a short nod, then hurried into the house.

"Daddy?"

The slamming of the back door was the only answer she got.

She stood in the dirt, fuming. He goes off for two days without a word, then comes home and ignores her? No way was she letting him get away with that. Plus, she had yet to tell him that she had canceled the ATM card.

Of course, his inability to withdraw cash from the bank could explain his lack of a greeting. With a heavy sigh, she trudged back to the house.

"Daddy?" He wasn't in the kitchen, nor in his room. "Daddy?" His bathroom was empty. She crossed through the living room to the small den they used as an office and found him booting up the computer. The screen desktop appeared and he clicked on the icon for the bookkeeping software.

Melanie's surprise was complete. Her father never looked at their finances. That was Melanie's area and had been for several years. As far as she knew, he'd never even used the accounting software before. "What are you doing?"

"What is this?" He stared at the computer screen.

"What is what?" She came and stood beside him to see what he was seeing. The pitifully low balance in their cash account. "It's a disaster is what it is."

"Where the hell's the rest of our money? And what nonsense is the bank spouting about us canceling our ATM card?"

Melanie folded her arms across her chest. "It's not nonsense. I canceled it yesterday. Along with our credit card."

He turned toward her as if in slow motion. His cheeks turned the color of fresh blood. "You *what?*"

Grown men had been known to back away from that look on his face. Melanie stood her ground. "I had no choice."

"What are you talking about? What happened to our bank balance?"

"What do you think happened to it?" she asked heatedly. "It went to pay off your damn bookie, and mother's never-ending spending sprees."

"What spending sprees?"

The entire subject made Melanie so angry her hands shook. She pulled out the credit card statement she'd received yesterday and tossed it at him. "Here's the latest fiasco. She maxed out the card. In one month she maxed it out. We can't pay it off. The interest charges alone are going to kill us. The two of you together are going to bankrupt us if you don't stop.''

Her father's eyes bulged. ''So you took it upon yourself to cancel our ATM and credit cards? Without consulting me?''

''I did what I had to do to keep us from going under. Granddad didn't build this ranch so we could put money in the pockets of bookies and boutiques.''

''We just sold our calves. Where's the money from that?''

''It's drawing interest, what's left of it, so we can pay the light bill for the rest of the year. You might remember that except for the occasional stud fee for Big Angus, there won't be any more income until we sell calves again next fall.''

''You watch your mouth, little girl. I've been ranching, running the PR since before you were born. I'm still your father and you'll by God do what I tell you. I need cash, and I need it right now, today. Or else.''

Melanie choked back the wail of misery and tears that threatened to burst from her. He was her father, and she loved him dearly. But she couldn't, wouldn't let him lose this ranch. If he was thinking straight, he would say she was right. As she saw it, it was her job to do what had to be done until this craziness that had a hold of him turned him loose.

''Or else what?'' she demanded, keeping her voice as hard and steady as she could. ''Or else what, Daddy?''

''You don't understand,'' he said earnestly. ''I need cash, and I need it now. Just five grand, that's all, I swear.''

''We don't have it to spare,'' she protested. ''You

can see that for yourself. The ranch can't afford any more of your gambling debts.''

"I swear," he said, "this is the last time, baby girl, the last time. I'll never gamble again."

"How many times have you said that? How many times have I fallen for it? The last time, I let you talk me into selling a prized bull, and now, here we are again. We've got only one prized bull left, and we're not selling him. If we sell Big Angus, we're finished. If we sell off part of the herd, we'll lose money—prices are way down right now. Even without this, we're looking at maybe not being able to make the balloon payment next year. With this, we're bankrupt, unless we want to sell land. Is that what you want us to do? Sell part of our land?"

"Come on," he protested. "It can't be that bad."

"Can't it? Look at these credit card bills from Mama's latest spree. Look at them. If we don't pay them, our credit is screwed."

He glanced irritably at the statement in his hand. Then his eyes widened as the figures jumped out at him. "Jeez, Louise, how could she have charged that much?"

"I don't know, but now you see what I mean. We can't pay it off this month." He obviously hadn't noticed that the largest charge was to a clinic. Melanie started to point it out, so he would know her mother was sick or hurt, but she decided not to. She didn't know for sure what was wrong with her mother. If it had been anything terrible, Aunt Karen would have called. Right now her dad was upset and under a great deal of stress. She would wait until she knew something definite about her mother before she told him.

"We're going to have to make payments and pay

sky-high interest,'' she said, ''and winter's coming on, which means we're going to have a nice fat heating bill every month.''

''I can't worry about things that haven't happened yet,'' he said. ''If I don't pay off Bruno by tomorrow they'll drill holes in my kneecaps—or worse—and that's the God's honest truth.''

Melanie shook her head at his exaggeration. ''No problem. We've still got medical insurance to cover that.''

''You think I'm joking?'' he cried.

''I think that if you take five thousand dollars out of our account, medical insurance will be one of the first things to go. Then it'll be the car insurance, the house insurance. Are you getting the picture yet? We spend an extra five thousand right now, we might as well hang it up, because we'll be finished.''

''Finished is right.'' He swore. ''If I don't pay him off I'll be finished.''

Melanie did her best to ignore the knot in her stomach. Tough love, she was learning, was at least as hard on the person dispensing it as on the recipient. This was killing her.

''You'll just have to find some other way to do it,'' she said. ''We don't have the money. I won't let your gambling bankrupt this ranch. I hope you understand.''

''Understand?'' he cried. ''I'm supposed to understand why my own flesh and blood is so selfish and tightfisted that she'd rather throw her own father to the wolves than turn loose of a few dollars?''

''Five thousand is not a few, and I'm not responsible for your gambling. You are. You did it, you fix it.''

''How? You've cut me off from my own money.''

''Your money? What am I? Chopped liver? A hired

hand? It was your idea to make me a partner. It was you and Mama together who decided I should have fifty percent while the two of you had a quarter each. You gave me the responsibility of keeping the PR solvent, and that's what I'm doing.''

His face turned from flushed to gray and back again. ''My own daughter.'' He shook his head and turned toward the door. ''It's not natural. It's just not natural.''

''Daddy?''

He stopped just beyond the doorway but did not turn back. ''I'm going out. I don't know when I'll be back. A day or two maybe.''

Melanie swallowed hard. Her vision blurred. ''Daddy?''

He kept walking. A moment later she heard the back door shut. His pickup started up, and he was gone.

''Oh, Daddy.'' She turned around and kicked the ottoman in front of the easy chair next to the desk. ''Dammit.''

''Was that your dad who just left?''

At the sound of Caleb's voice from the doorway Melanie bit back a groan. ''Yes.''

She heard him move closer. ''He didn't stay long,'' he said. ''Is he coming back?''

Melanie found that she couldn't turn around. Couldn't face her best friend. She hated family discord, hated even more that she had told Caleb about her father's gambling, their financial troubles. It was too embarrassing. No, she couldn't turn around.

But she wanted to. Wanted to turn around and lean on him, let him prop her up until she felt steady enough to cope again. She wanted it so much that she steeled herself against even looking at him.

''He said he'd be gone a day or two.''

"Mel?" He put a hand on her shoulder. "Are you all right?"

"Yeah. Fine. Listen…" She forced herself to turn and smile. "Thanks for offering to stick around and help, but I'll be fine. You can go on home." And she could take a run out to the hay field and pound on a bale or two. If she didn't get to hit something, and soon, she was going to explode. Or cry. Neither, as far as she was concerned, was acceptable in front of Caleb.

"We've already had this argument, and you lost. I'm staying."

On the other hand, she thought, there were an awful lot of bales to be loaded and stored in the hay barn. Twenty acres' worth. It was normally a three-person job. With Caleb's help, the two of them should be able to get the work done today. Alone it would take her two or three days, if she didn't kill herself in the process. It was a nasty, dirty job, almost as bad as cutting the hay in the first place, with bits of hay finding their way inside a person's clothes and making you itch to high heaven.

"All right." She gave him a nod. "But we're loading and hauling hay and there's only two of us, so don't say I didn't warn you."

"Fair enough."

Caleb was just glad she'd given in, since he'd had no intention of leaving her alone to fend for herself. He was only sorry he hadn't caught Ralph before the man had disappeared again. That man needed his butt kicked.

Chapter Four

Caleb and Melanie had worked together many times over the years, helping out at each other's ranch, or on someone else's ranch. They worked together now with few words, as few were necessary. Each knew what needed to be done.

They started in the kitchen, making lunch to take with them. They pulled everything they wanted from the refrigerator and spread it on the table, then walked around it building sandwiches. A regular assembly line of sandwich production. They had bread, mustard and mayonnaise, lettuce and tomatoes and sliced cheese. Roast beef and bologna, peanut butter and jelly.

"You got enough mayo there?"

Caleb looked up from where he was spreading mayonnaise on a slice of bread. "I like mayo."

"I do, too, but I still want to taste the meat when I bite in."

"Who's doing this, you or me?"

"You, but I have to eat it."

"Wimp." He scraped a thick layer of mayo from the slice before him. "Is that better?"

"Yes. Thank you."

"And don't skimp on the peanut butter."

"I'm not," she protested.

"Are too."

She slathered it on as thick as she could. "Better?"

"Yes, thank you."

"The fine art of compromise," she said.

With half a dozen sandwiches stacked on the table, Melanie turned back toward the refrigerator and found Caleb doing the same. He reached the door first and pulled it open. He went for the apples while she retrieved two bananas.

Melanie stepped to the pantry and tossed him a roll of plastic wrap for the sandwiches. While he wrapped, she found a big bag of potato chips to add to their lunch. As he wrapped the last sandwich she hauled out the small cooler from the floor of the pantry and they started piling everything in, except the bag of chips, which wouldn't fit. They packed a second cooler with ice and cans of soft drinks, and grabbed two tall plastic tumblers for drinking water from the jug on the truck.

On their way out the door Melanie grabbed her old leather work gloves and a ball cap to keep her hair from blowing in her face.

"Do you need anything?" she asked him.

"Gloves and hat in my rig."

While he retrieved those items she carried the coolers and chips to the big equipment shed. She set her load down on a bench and opened the wide doors. "Hello, Sister."

Caleb was just coming up behind her and laughed. "I'd forgotten you call that old truck Sister."

"*Old* being the operative word. Daddy brought her home brand spanking new about three years before I was born. Which is how she came to be his first baby. That makes her my sister."

The old truck had been manufactured specifically for hauling hay. Basically, it was a wooden bed, twenty-five-feet long by eight-and-a-half wide, on wheels. The engine, instead of being under a hood in the front, was mounted dead center beneath the bed, mere inches above the ground. Woe be unto the driver who hit a deep hole or rut.

Been there, done that, Melanie thought. Still had the memory of her daddy's cussing to prove it.

Rather than a cab like on a regular truck or pickup, Sister had a driver's station on the left front corner of the bed, complete with seat, steering wheel, gearshift, pedals, and control panel. When Melanie was a baby her dad built an enclosure—only a cover, really, with open sides—to offer a modicum of shade and protection for the driver. He had also mounted a large, insulated water jug, which had to be replaced every five years or so, as the sun and weather broke it down, on the right front corner of the bed. It made a handy passenger seat.

When Melanie had started driving the truck for her dad she'd barely been twelve. Her mother had insisted that Ralph install a seat belt for her. The belt was still there.

Whoever sat on the water jug, however, was on his own.

A loading conveyor extended off the front of the truck, with another conveyor running down the middle of the truck bed. As the truck was driven through the field, one bale at a time would be scooped up by the front conveyor, carried up to the second conveyor, which took it down the bed toward the rear guard that kept it from falling off the back.

Ordinarily two people worked together picking the bales off the second belt and stacking them on the bed, from back to front, until the load was full. The truck could carry one-hundred-fifty square bales of approximately sixty-five pounds each. Nine-thousand-seven-hundred and fifty pounds of dry grass.

Today, instead of one to drive and two to do the toting and stacking, there would be one to drive, one to stack. And it would probably take them two loads to clear the field. Scoop it up, stack it, haul it to the hay barn, unload it, restack it. Go back to the field and do it all again. Melanie would make sure they traded off several times. No way was she going to have Caleb doing all that work himself. Especially after she had clobbered him in the shoulder that morning.

While Caleb rinsed and filled the big water jug on the truck Melanie got the toolbox from the shed and slid it in behind the driver's seat. They checked the gas tank, found it full, and Melanie climbed into the driver's seat.

Caleb frowned.

"What?" she asked, her lips twitching.

"I thought I'd drive," Caleb said.

"Did you, now? And why is that?"

He bit the inside of his jaw. "Habit? Never mind."

"You offered to help," she told him. "Tell me I'm not going to be butting up against your he-man ego all day."

His eyes widened. "My what? I don't have a he-man ego. Whatever the hell that is. When have I ever tried to stop you from doing anything you wanted to do?''

"How about that time I wanted to drive Jerry MacKenzie's motorcycle in high school? You had long since graduated. Just what were you doing in the school parking lot that day?''

"I was saving your hide. That motorcycle was a death trap, and you weren't even going to wear a helmet.''

"I suppose you wear a helmet when you ride a horse, which is a darn sight more unpredictable than a motorcycle.''

"A horse doesn't have anywhere near the torque that a Harley does.''

"Did you ever ride a Harley?'' she asked pointedly.

"We're not talking about me.''

"Oh, yeah, the old double standard.''

"You were a seventeen-year-old kid.''

She started the truck and put it in gear. "Don't you mean girl?''

"If the shoe fits, Cinderella.''

"Oh, ugh.''

"What? I thought girls liked Cinderella.''

"Sure.'' She headed for the first of several gates they would have to open to get through, then close behind them to keep cattle and horses in their pastures. On horseback, gates could be fun, a challenge. You leaned down from the saddle without dismounting and opened a gate, rode through, then closed and latched it behind you. No big deal. At least not the first seven hundred times you did it. After that it was just a necessary nuisance.

In a vehicle it was a royal pain in the tush, especially if you were alone. Drive up, stop, get out, push the gate all the way open and make sure it doesn't swing shut. Drive through, stop, get out, walk back to the gate, realize you didn't drive through far enough to close the gate, get back in and pull forward, get out and walk back, close and latch the gate, walk back to the truck. A pain in the tush.

"Cinderella was a great role model for little girls," she informed him. "She got her heart's desire not by having to work for it, but by having small feet. Gives every little girl something worthwhile to strive for, don't you think? Teaches a valuable lesson about life."

He scrunched up his face. "Small feet?"

"Forget it." She pulled to a stop. "Passenger gets the gates."

He scowled. "That's why you wanted to drive."

"Of course."

She watched as he got out and walked to the gate. Sauntered was more like it, with a cute little bobble and wave from the leather work gloves, the fingers of which were sticking out of his right hip pocket.

Hello, gloves.

Hello, nice butt.

She blinked and found him standing there holding the gate open, a puzzled look on his face as he stared back at her.

Oops. Caught, she thought. Better keep her mind on the business at hand. Which meant keeping her mind off Caleb, which was going to be hard to do, since they were going to be joined at the hip, so to speak, all day.

She drove through the open gate and idled, waiting while Caleb closed the gate and climbed back onto the water jug he was using as a seat. They repeated the process three more times before reaching the far hay field.

The sky was a clear, cloudless blue. The angle of light and shadow where the woods met the field spoke of fall. The breeze carried that sweet, pungent perfume of twenty acres of freshly cut alfalfa.

Melanie scanned the field, then looked at Caleb.

"I'm betting we can get all this stored in the hay barn before dark," he said.

"How's your shoulder?" she asked.

"It's fine." He stood up and tugged on his gloves. "Just drive. I'll stack."

"I can stack bales," she said.

"I'm sure you can. But you wanted to drive."

"All right," she said. "But I'll spell you."

"We'll see."

Melanie drove the big lumbering truck straight and slowly down each row of bales, aiming the end of the loader at each next bale. The conveyor belt carried the bale back to the truck bed where Caleb added it to the growing stack.

The day was warm for October. Mother Nature decided to give them a late dose of summer and pushed the temperature up into the mid eighties, which wasn't necessarily hot, unless your body protested that, *Hey, it's October already, cool it down some, will ya?* The heat, Melanie realized, was both a curse and a blessing. A curse because lifting and stacking bales was hot, heavy work even in cool weather; now it made the sweat roll. A blessing because the warmth had Caleb taking off his shirt before they made it to the second row. The T-shirt he wore beneath it hugged every curve and dip and bulge in his muscled shoulders and torso.

Nice, she thought. Very, very nice.

When Melanie made the turn at the end of the fourth row she had just enough time to notice that one of the old wooden fence posts was down and the wires sagging when the loading conveyor jerked and let out a squeal, then made a hideous grinding noise before it stopped altogether. Melanie shut it down immediately then killed the truck engine. The acrid stench of burning rubber stung her nostrils.

She jumped left off the truck; Caleb leaped off the right side. They met on opposite sides of the loading conveyor.

"If we can't fix this thing," Melanie muttered, "Daddy's going to have my head on a platter." Heaven knew she was already in the running for his least favorite person of the year after this morning. "I smelled burning rubber."

"Me, too." Caleb knelt at the front end of the loader.

"But I smell wood smoke, too." She noted the turn she'd just made, next to the fence. A thick stand of scrub oak grew on the other side of the barbed wire, with dozens of limbs hanging over. "Could have picked up a small limb."

Caleb looked up at her. "Only one way to tell."

"I'll get the toolbox."

"You notice the fence there?" he called.

"Yeah, I saw it. One problem at a time. I'll get the fence tomorrow."

By working together they loosened the tension on the conveyor and found a mass of twigs caught up in a place it shouldn't be. The clump had managed to get caught in just the wrong spot to gum up the works. They had it cleaned out and the belt operating smoothly in minutes.

"Oh, we're good." Melanie put the tools they'd used back into the toolbox.

"Never doubt it," Caleb said. He met her gaze, held it. His voice deepened. Softened. "We make a good team."

Melanie couldn't have looked away if she had tried. She felt mesmerized, held captive by the questions in his eyes, questions she didn't understand.

He put out his hand. "Put it there, partner."

Melanie blinked and, in slow motion, reached for his hand. If, on contact, she flinched slightly at the sharp charge of electricity that raced up her arm, well, maybe that was okay, because he flinched, too.

They broke contact.

Caleb's lips quirked. "That just keeps happening to us."

Melanie reminded herself that she didn't intend to screw up their friendship. Just then, looking into his deep brown eyes, she wasn't sure why—oh, yeah. Best friend she'd ever had. Only person she could be herself with. Okay. Okay. She wouldn't let a little fact like heated blood and tingling skin make her do something, something else, anyway, to damage their friendship.

"You drive." She grabbed the toolbox and turned back toward the truck. "I'll stack for a while."

Caleb started to argue. There was no need for her to lift and stack bales of hay. He wasn't tired, wasn't likely to get that way anytime soon, and wasn't likely to keel over dead if he did get tired.

But he'd seen that *don't argue with me, my mind's made up* look in her eyes when she had turned away.

Hell with it. If she wanted to wear herself out, who was he to stop her?

If, in the back of his mind, he knew that he had never before—before he'd gotten a good solid taste of her Saturday night, and last night, and this morning—if he'd never worried about her working too hard and wearing herself out, well, that was something to think about. Later.

Caleb drove the truck, and Melanie found her rhythm stacking bales. Slip fingers beneath baling wire. Grab, lift, swing, stack. Pull hands out from beneath baling wire. Turn. Do it all again. Honest work that taxed the muscles and worked up a sweat. Mindless work that left the brain free to wander. Hers wanted to wander to her friend in the driver's seat.

She blanked her mind and thought instead of her father, wondered where he was, when he would be back. She thought of her mother, wondered how she was, when she would call.

Then she thought of nothing at all except lifting the next bale.

They didn't yet have a full load when Caleb suggested they take what they had to the hay barn and come back for the rest.

Melanie would have argued, despite the growing ache in her hands and muscles, but she could see that they'd already loaded more than half the field, but they couldn't get all of the rest of it this trip. It would take a second load, regardless.

Besides, she was hungry.

Caleb drove to the hay barn in the pasture beyond the hay field while Melanie sat on the water jug and let the slight breeze dry the sweat on her face. At the barn Melanie jumped down and opened the doors so Caleb could back the truck in.

"You want to eat first?" Caleb asked once he stopped and killed the engine. "Or unload?"

"Eat," she said. "I'm starving."

They carried their coolers to the hay bales already stacked in the barn, then Melanie darted back to the truck.

"Wait," she said, digging into the toolbox. A moment later she was back at his side handing him a moistened towelette in a packet.

Caleb smirked. "Afraid of a little dirt?"

"We're civilized here on the PR. We wash up before we eat."

"You carry these things in the toolbox?"

"Why not?"

Caleb shrugged and tore the end off the packet. "Shrimpfest?"

"They give them out at the all-you-can-eat fish place up in the city."

"And you bring them home."

"Whatever works."

As soon as their hands were clean they dived in. After the first sandwich and two full cups of water Melanie felt better. She let out a long sigh, certain now that she was in no danger of starving to death.

"Tell me something pleasant," she said.

He plucked an apple out of the cooler. "What would you consider pleasant?"

"Oh, I don't know. How is it having a woman and two kids living in the house these days? Are you guys used to them yet?"

Caleb chuckled. "Sloan is."

"Do tell. I'm sure he's happy as a lark. Must put a crimp in your style, though, and Justin's."

"Well, we don't walk around the house in our underwear. Or out of it. But then, Grandmother would have boxed our ears if we'd ever done it once we passed the age of about four, women and girls around or not."

"So it's no big deal, then, having a woman and two little girls around."

"Are you kidding? It's great. Emily makes these great desserts, and there's always fresh-baked cookies of one kind or another in the kitchen, and fresh flowers all over the house. And those girls, they're so cute you just want to hug 'em."

"Food and fun," she said with a smirk. "Is that what it takes to please a man? Comfort and entertainment." She shook her head. "Which would explain why I'm not married."

Caleb bit into his apple and chewed thoughtfully.

Melanie frowned. "The fruit's supposed to be dessert."

"Why aren't you married?" he asked. "If you're really not still hung up on Sloan—"

"If?" She gaped at him. "What do you mean, if?"

"I don't know." He shrugged and unwrapped another sandwich. Roast beef this time. "I guess I've been thinking lately that maybe you aren't as over him as you thought you were." He shrugged again. "Maybe I was wrong."

"No maybe about it." Suddenly it became more important than ever that he believe her. "You know I've been over him for a long, long time. You *know* that."

"I thought I knew that." He studied his sandwich

as if trying to figure out what it was and how it got into his hand. ''Until the other night at the party.''

''I told you I had a lot on my mind but that it had nothing to do with Sloan.''

''Yeah.'' He looked her in the eye. ''And then you kissed me.''

Heat stung her cheeks. ''Next time I'll just let the barracuda have you.''

''Then you went out two nights later and got yourself drunk. That's not like you, Mel.''

''No,'' she agreed. ''It's not like me. I didn't set out to get drunk, you know. I just kept thinking about the money and Daddy's gambling and Mama's bills, and I just kept drinking. Stupid.''

''You'll get no argument from me.''

She made a face. ''I can always count on you for comfort and support.''

''Hey, what are friends for?''

Melanie grabbed a banana from the cooler and pulled the peel down. She was losing her appetite fast. She ate her banana in silence, then dropped the peel into the cooler.

''I've had enough. I'll get started.'' She climbed onto the truck and started tossing bales to the ground.

Caleb ate a third sandwich in four quick bites. If he lived to be a hundred he would never understand women. He had thought, for most of his life, that he knew this one, understood her mind and heart. But since Saturday she had done nothing but confound him time after time.

He'd even confounded himself a time or two in regards to her.

And if she threw those bales down any harder she was going to dislocate a shoulder.

One thing he did know when it came to women. No matter the situation, a man could never go wrong with an apology. Didn't matter if there was anything to apologize for. A man had nearly always done something wrong. In the eyes of a woman.

He cleaned up the remains of their lunch and stowed the coolers back on the truck, then climbed up with Melanie, who kept her back turned and ignored him.

"Melanie." He waited until she had tossed the bale she held, then put his hands on her shoulders. "Melanie, I'm sorry."

She whipped her head around, surprise written across her face. "For what?"

He turned her until she stood facing him, and brushed his fingers along her cheek. "I didn't mean to upset you. I'm just, I don't know, trying to figure things out, I guess."

She stared up at him, her green eyes clouded with questions. "What kinds of things?"

Overhead a carpenter bee buzzed loudly as it drilled a hole in a wooden beam, and from farther up in the rafters came the flutter of wings. Caleb didn't look up to see what kind of bird intruded on them. Probably a pigeon.

"Things," he said, "like why we all of a sudden seem to end up kissing every time we turn around."

Her throat worked on a swallow. "Kissing?"

"Yeah." He leaned closer. "You know, your lips, my lips, lightning bolts."

Something skittered across her face, through her eyes, that looked suspiciously like fear. "Good grief." She stepped back and laughed. Nervously. "Not here. With our track record we'd set the hay on fire. Let's get back to work."

He wanted, badly, to ask her what that look had meant. She couldn't be afraid of him. Not him. It wasn't possible.

But she lifted another bale and tossed it down. She wasn't going to talk. Not now.

That didn't mean he intended to let the matter drop for long. Not when all he could think about was kissing her again.

They finished unloading and stacking the bales, then drove back to the field to get the rest. When Caleb moved to the back of the truck to start stacking, Melanie didn't object. He was bigger and stronger than she was. She'd be an idiot to try to match him bale for bale.

Besides, all she had to do was readjust her rearview mirror slightly and she could watch those beautiful biceps flex and bulge. Best view in the county.

She wondered if she'd ever before seen that particular lock of black hair fall from beneath his cowboy hat at just that angle across his forehead. In defense against the urge to walk back there and smooth it back from his face, she gripped the steering wheel tighter.

There was no use trying to talk over the rumble of the engine while Caleb worked in the back and Melanie sat in the driver's seat, but they didn't find much to say to each other later, either, when they returned to the hay barn or while they unloaded, or during the drive back to the house.

Melanie knew they wouldn't be using the truck again until next season, so instead of pulling into the equipment shed she stopped in the yard.

"Drain the water jug?" Caleb asked.

"You read my mind."

"I'll get it." There was enough water left that letting it drain out the tap would have taken several minutes. Instead he unstrapped the jug, opened the top and dumped the water in the flower bed beside the house.

Melanie gathered up the coolers from lunch and carried them to the house while Caleb backed the truck into the shed. He met her in the kitchen where she was cleaning up the coolers.

"I really appreciate all your work today," she told him.

"You're welcome, but you know you don't have to thank me. You'd do the same if I had a need."

"Of course I would. Still, I'm grateful. If I'd had to do that job alone it would have taken me days, and who knows what the weather might do before Daddy comes home."

"I was glad to help."

"I was glad to have you."

"Are we through yet?"

She blinked. "Through with what?"

"With whatever this polite, I-barely-know-you-but-thanks-anyway nonsense is."

This time she blinked twice. "I don't know what you're talking about."

"Okay, fine." He threw his hands in the air. "But if that look of fear I see in your eyes is for me you're really going to piss me off, pal."

"You think I'm afraid of you?" she cried.

He wished he knew if the outrage on her face was real or feigned. He suddenly felt as if he was walking through a minefield where she was concerned.

"You're afraid of something," he said. "Every time I've been near you today you get this look of panic in your eyes. Maybe I've come on a little strong a couple of times, but for crying out loud, Melanie, this is *me.* You have to know I'd cut off my right arm before I'd hurt you.''

"Good grief." Melanie gaped. "You think I don't know that?"

"For the past few days, when it comes to you I don't know what to think." But he breathed easier.

"Well, there you have it. We're in total agreement. This whole…whatever it is…is just crazy. We need to go back to the way things were."

"Were?"

"You know. Before."

"Before what?"

"You know."

"What's the matter, can't you even say it? We kissed. More than once."

"I don't need to say it. You're saying it enough for both of us."

"And you're avoiding the subject entirely. Except for last night."

"Now you're throwing last night in my face?"

"Absolutely not," he argued, fighting a grin. He didn't care how mad she got as long as she wasn't indifferent.

With narrowed eyes, she tapped her toe and folded her arms across her chest. "I'm glad we got that cleared up. Now, as grateful as I am for your help today, I've got things to do. Give your grandmother my best, and say hi to Emily and the girls."

"I'll do that. When I call home later."

"When you—" She planted her hands on her hips. "Go home, Caleb."

"Not gonna happen," he said. "I don't see your dad around here anywhere, and I'm not about to go off and leave you here, isolated and alone, when you've had strangers snooping around the place.''

Melanie opened her mouth to protest, but then she remembered her father saying he needed to pay off a man named Bruno. Bruno. It could be that Caleb was more correct than he'd realized when he'd called her snooping strangers thumb breakers.

Bruno, for crying out loud. She was just worried enough to shut her mouth on further protests of Caleb's intentions of staying.

But there was no sense in giving in too easily and giving him a swelled head.

''I didn't notice any strangers out there when we came in.''

''I'm staying. If you weren't so stubborn you'd agree it's a good idea.''

''Stubborn. I'm stubborn?''

''If the shoe fits—''

''If you call me Cinderella again, I might have to hurt you.''

''I'm shaking in my boots.''

''You should be. Stubborn. This from a man they call *yanasa*.''

''Aw, come on. Don't start that.''

His family had given him the nickname when he'd been a kid. The Cherokee word meant buffalo. His grandmother and brothers said it fit him because he was about as immovable as that hairy beast.

''Gotcha.'' She gave him a cheesy grin. ''Well, don't just stand there, go get cleaned up for supper. But you're doing the dishes.''

His smile was slow and devastating. ''I've got no problem with that.''

That smile was all it took to make her pulse spike.

* * *

There were a few more chores to do after supper. Caleb tagged along and helped gather eggs, lock up the chickens to keep the coyotes and possums from getting them, bring the mares back into the stable and give them some grain.

Afterward Melanie told Caleb to make himself at home while she did some paperwork at the desk in the den. She heard him turn on the television while she made note of the final hay load. Unless they had the worst winter on record—and the way the PR's luck was going, that was entirely possible—there should be plenty of hay to see the cattle and horses through the winter.

She smiled as a feminine Southern drawl came from the television in the living room. "As God is my witness, I'll never be hungry again."

Then she heard Caleb change channels.

She was in the living room and grabbing the remote from his hand in under three seconds.

"You can't do that," she cried, changing the channel back.

He looked at her as if she'd lost her mind. "Jeez, sorry. All I did was change channels. You weren't even in here."

"You did a lot more than change channels. You committed a supreme no-no."

"Let me guess. You're on medication and you missed your last dose."

"You are *sooo* funny."

"I'm glad one of us is. Supreme no-no," he muttered.

"Supreme no-no," she repeated. "The top three supreme no-nos would be, you never turn your back while the flag is being raised, you never walk out during 'Amazing Grace,' and you never change channels during *Gone With the Wind*.''

"I won't change the channel, if you sit here and watch it with me."

"Good enough."

"Do we get popcorn?" he asked hopefully.

Despite brushing and flossing, she was still picking popcorn hulls out of her teeth hours later when she went to bed.

Sleep, however, eluded her. How was she supposed to relax when she knew that Caleb was only a few feet away, across the hall in the spare bedroom? How was she supposed to close her eyes when every time she did she kept seeing that errant lock of hair fall forward onto his sweat-dampened forehead?

How was she supposed to sleep when he hadn't tried to kiss her again?

She rolled her face into her pillow to muffle a groan of frustration. She was out of her mind. Perverse. Crazy. Stupid. She wanted to kiss him again. Wanted, maybe, more than that. Yet when the opportunity arose, she pushed him away, or ran.

Stupid.

But why did her best friend suddenly have to be so damn appealing?

Caleb didn't have as much trouble going to sleep as Melanie did. But once he slept, he dreamed. About green eyes, dark hair, smooth skin. No fear in those eyes, but warmth, welcome. The afternoon in the hay barn, in his dream, was spent much differently than the reality. They had, indeed, set the hay on fire. Figuratively speaking.

Beneath his rough fingers her skin felt like silk. Beneath her touch his skin felt on fire.

In the dream there had been no need to work buttons, fumble with zippers. Their clothing melted away, letting the warm air caress every inch of them, as they caressed, tasted, every inch of each other.

He took her down onto the fresh, fragrant hay. In his dream it was loose and soft rather than baled and prickly. She reached for him and pulled him down into heaven.

He woke at 3:00 a.m., hot and hard and sweaty.

He nearly laughed out loud. He hadn't wanted a woman this badly in a long time, and it felt good. Damn good. Too bad he couldn't do anything about it.

Of course, he had options, but they were limited.

He could knock on Melanie's door and hope she didn't keep a gun in her bedroom.

Naw, bad idea.

He could take a cold shower, as distasteful as that sounded. But the noise of the shower would probably wake Melanie, and how would he explain taking a shower at 3:00 a.m.?

In frustration, he rolled over and buried his face in his pillow to stifle a groan.

The next morning started out more calmly than the one before. No hangovers, no hitting each other with shovels. No breath-stealing kiss in the kitchen. Just bacon and eggs and pancakes.

While Melanie started breakfast, Caleb headed for the back door.

"Where are you going?" she asked.

"I thought I'd turn the mares out."

"Why don't you cook and I'll take care of the mares."

"The whole point of my being here is so you don't go out to the barn, or anywhere else, alone, in case those goons come back."

"But it's okay for you to go alone? I don't think so."

"Come on, Melanie, you're—"

"If you were about to say I'm a girl—"

"I wouldn't dream of it. We'll eat, then go out together."

"A very sensible plan. How do you want your eggs?"

With breakfast behind them and the kitchen cleaned up, they headed out for the day. They let the chickens out, then the mares, and cleaned out the stalls. Every step Melanie took, Caleb was right beside her. They invariably reached for the same bucket, the rake, the pitchfork at the same time, ending up tangling their fingers together more than once.

By the time they finished in the barn Melanie was almost used to the constant tingling that shot up her arm every time their hands touched.

She started to complain. There was plenty of room, no need for him to crowd her so damn much. But she had the feeling he was just waiting for her to gripe at him. She decided not to give him the satisfaction.

They loaded fencing supplies—T-posts, post pounder, wire, come-along, fencing pliers, staples, and more—into the back of her pickup and followed the path they had driven the day before to the field where the fence needed repairing.

They installed a new T-post halfway between the broken wooden post and the next post on either side, took out the broken one and restrung the barbed wire, fastening it securely to the new posts.

It was inevitable, with two people working together on such a chore, for their shoulders to occasionally brush, their knees to bump, their hands to touch. Accidentally, of course. Every touch an accident. Almost every touch.

Sometimes, however, he was a little too casual about it, telling Melanie that some of the touching was on purpose. Such as when he reached across her for the fencing pliers and his forearm brushed slowly, lightly against hers.

Sharp tingles of awareness flooded her. Her nipples peaked. Her breath caught.

"Sorry," he said.

Melanie wasn't buying it. He looked entirely too innocent.

All right, *pal,* she thought. Two can play this game. "No problem," she told him quietly. "Oh, no!" she cried as she smeared dirt all down his arm. Accidentally, of course. "Now I'm the one who's sorry. Here, let me." She stripped off her gloves and gently stroked the dirty spot.

He jumped as though he'd been shot. "It's just dirt. Leave it."

"No, I think there's a scratch under there. It could get infected." She reached into the toolbox and pulled out one of her packaged towelettes. "This'll just take a second."

But instead of wiping off the dirt, Melanie cradled his forearm in one hand and used the other to caress the soiled skin. She brushed carefully from elbow to wrist, barely touching, applying no pressure. Then she did it again, sideways, following the pattern of hair growth, inner arm to outer, inner to outer.

His arm jerked in her hand, but he didn't pull away. She did, however, hear him swallow rather heavily.

She had to fight to keep from doing the same. Her ploy to tease him seemed to be backfiring, if the spike in her pulse was any indication. The sight of her pale hands on his bronze skin made her heart pound.

"There." Her voice was a little too breathy for comfort. "All clean, and no cut at all."

He swallowed again, cleared his throat as he turned away. "Thanks."

He didn't brush or bump or rub against her again. It didn't seem to matter. She was as aware of him as if he were stroking her bare flesh.

They finished the repairs, then drove along the fence checking for any other trouble spots. They found a place where a tree had fallen and pulled the fence between the PR and the Cherokee Rose down with it. It was just lucky that neither ranch had any cattle nearby.

As they hauled out their supplies again, Caleb said, "I can't believe in all these years we haven't just put a gate in this fence so we can go back and forth when we want."

Melanie paused and looked at him. Then at the fence. "I've thought the same thing a dozen times over the years," she admitted.

"Why didn't you say something?"

She shrugged. "I don't know. I guess I thought it was a dumb idea."

"What's dumb about it?"

She shrugged again. "Nothing, now that I think about it."

He grinned at her. "You game?"

She grinned back. "Why not? We could rig a Texas gate out of wire." A Texas gate consisted of strands of wire fastened to a stationary fence post at one end and a loose, unplanted post at the other. Loops of wire on the opposite post held the loose post in place to close the gate. Simple, effective.

"Let's do it," Caleb said.

She laughed. "What's Sloan going to say?"

"Or your dad," Caleb said.

"Hey, if he can't take a joke, to heck with him. Besides," she added grimly, "he can't get much madder at me than he already is."

Caleb rested a hand on her shoulder. "Don't worry, the two of you will work it out."

She gave him a wry smile. "Are you sure?"

"Of course I am." He turned her and held her gently by both shoulders. "You and your dad are closer than any other two people I know. He's worried about his debt, you're worried about the ranch. You'll work it out."

"I hope you're right."

"I know I am. And you know he won't mind about the gate."

She smiled. "No, he won't mind."

"Well, then, let's get it done."

Chapter Five

It was another long night for Melanie, but the reasons were somehow different from the night before. Today, not only had she felt the sharp physical pull toward Caleb, the hot sexual tension, but she'd also been reminded of his kindness, and his sense of fun.

How was a woman supposed to resist all of that? Why would a sane one even want to try?

She must have eventually fallen asleep—although she had seen 2:00 a.m. come and go on her bedside clock—because she woke at her usual five o'clock.

Bleary eyed, she stumbled from the bed and down the hall to the shower. Ten minutes of hot water pounding on her head helped make her feel more like a human being. She put on her robe, shoved her wet hair back with her hands and opened the bathroom door.

And ran smack into the hard wall of Caleb's chest.

"Oomph," was the closest way to describe the

sound she made. Yet even with most of the breath knocked out of her she had no trouble feeling the solid warmth of his bare chest against her face and hands as she tried to catch herself.

"Whoa." Caleb stepped back and steadied her by clasping her arms. "Sorry. Guess I was still half-asleep. Are you all right?"

"I'm fine." Or she would be, if she could convince her hands to remove themselves from his pecs. Oh, the man had glorious pecs.

"You sure?" he asked, his fingers flexing on her upper arms. "You look a little dazed."

She caught herself leaning closer to him and jumped back. "I just haven't had my coffee yet. I'll, uh, go start breakfast while you shower."

Caleb turned and watched as she beat a hasty retreat to her bedroom. He entered the bathroom and closed the door, taking in the scent of her soap and shampoo that lingered in the air.

That was no lack of coffee he'd seen in her eyes. She was just glad to see him, or his name wasn't Caleb Chisholm.

By the time he stepped into the shower, he was whistling.

"What's on today's agenda?" he asked over breakfast.

Melanie had given herself a stern lecture while she dressed and another while she cooked. Caleb was her friend, and he had volunteered to help her around the ranch. If she didn't get a grip on herself she would end up drooling all over him, and wouldn't that be a pretty sight?

But she was steady now, and prepared to act normally around him. If it killed her.

"Since you're here and willing to work, I thought we'd saddle up and move the Angus herd up to the corral for their worming. You know, the glamorous part of ranching."

"Well," he offered with a slight smirk. "The riding might be glamorous, but I'd have to argue about the worming."

An hour later they were saddled up and riding toward the pasture where the purebred Angus herd grazed. There were only a dozen head of the black cattle, not counting the bull, Big Angus, who was kept in a separate pasture.

It was a glorious morning, warm and bright, the smell of cottonwood leaves turning for the season teasing the air. The call of bob-white quail was music on the breeze, with a counterpoint of the creak of leather, a cow calling her calf.

"If there's any better life than this," she said, staring up at the blue, blue sky, "I can't imagine what it could be."

"There is no better," Caleb said.

They rode on at a walk, in silence. Melanie felt an emotional closeness with Caleb that she'd never felt before. At times like this she believed they were more than friends, they were kindred spirits, two people with like values who enjoyed the same things, believed in the same things.

"Mind if I ask you a question?" Caleb said.

She tilted her face to the sky and took in a deep breath. "Right now I feel so good you can ask me anything you want."

"It's personal, and maybe none of my business."

"Oh boy, this ought to be good. Go ahead. Shoot. I might even answer it."

"If you don't want to, that's okay. If the subject makes you uncomfortable we can drop it."

She peered over at him. "Now you've got my curiosity up."

He gave a slight shrug and gazed out over toward the woods on the far side of the empty pasture they were crossing.

"It's about Sloan."

Melanie laughed. "He's your brother. I doubt there's anything I can tell you that you don't already know."

"Except why you finally gave up on him when you say you did a couple of years ago."

"When I say I did?" she cried. "You still don't believe me?"

"Don't get your drawers in a twist. I'm—"

"Drawers in a *twist?*"

"—just trying to figure it out in my head and I don't get it. One day you were chasing after him, crying when he wouldn't return your feelings, the next you're saying you're over him. How does that work?"

Melanie came close to telling him to mind his own business, but considering how many times over the years she had used his shoulder for a crying pillow, it seemed as though the subject of her feelings for Sloan pretty much was Caleb's business. As close as she and Caleb had been all their lives, there was plenty she had never told him. Maybe it was time she did.

"When I was five years old Freddie Wilson threw me out into the middle of that pond over at your place. We were having a picnic or something. Maybe Fourth of July."

"I remember," Caleb said. "Sloan fished you out. What does that have to do with your getting over him?"

"I'm telling this," she said. "Anyway, he didn't just fish me out. He saved me."

"Saved you, hell. That water didn't even come up to your chin."

"Yes, but I didn't know that. I was a good swimmer, but I thought the whole pond was as shallow in the middle as it was two feet from shore. When Freddie, the creep, threw me in I went under and came up spitting red, dirty water. My mother had tied my hair in pigtails, and I had these pretty, red-white-and-blue ribbons. Now they were ruined. I was so mad I wanted to scream. And my knee hurt where I'd scraped it on something. When I went to stand up I kept my leg bent, but the bottom wasn't where I thought it should be, so I went under again."

"And Sloan saved you."

"From my earliest memories my mother used to read to me. Fairy tales."

He chuckled. "'Cinderella'?"

"Among others. Stories of knights on white steeds riding to the rescue of damsels in distress. The darkly handsome prince, older, wiser, a man of the world, saving the fair young maiden."

"I'm sure I heard some of those same stories, growing up."

"Maybe, but you guys get to be the knights and princes. You get to fight the battles, slay the dragons, defeat the villains and save the girl. For the most part, the girl—Cinderella, Snow White, Sleeping Beauty, whoever—is supposed to look pretty even in rags, keep a clean house, prepare gourmet food from scraps, always be a lady, and wait to be rescued by the man of her dreams.''

''What about Goldilocks? She had an adventure.''

Melanie shrugged. ''She broke into a house, ate someone else's food and went to sleep. She didn't get to climb a beanstalk and face down a giant. She didn't get to wield a sword to defeat some deadly monster. She ate and went to sleep.''

''Okay, okay. Small feet and looking pretty. I get it.''

''I doubt it, but anyway, there I was, five years old and thinking I was drowning. Then, out of the blue appears this beautiful, dark-skinned older man of thirteen. He wasn't riding a white steed, but his bay was tied up to a tree at the edge of the pond. He waded in and lifted me out of the water with one arm. One arm. The only other person I knew of who was that strong was my father. Daddy had always been my hero. But that day Sloan took over the title. I was, as they say, smitten.''

''Sloan was your knight.''

''And my prince. And my hero.''

''Is there a point to this regarding getting over him?''

''I'm getting to it. Don't get your drawers in a twist,'' she added with a smirk.

''Touché.''

''Anyway, when I got home from the picnic all I could talk about was Sloan. If I'd been about ten years older I might have recognized the gleam that came into my mother's eyes, but I didn't. I just thought she was as excited about Sloan as I was. And in truth, she was.''

''She liked the idea of your needing to be rescued from the pond?''

"No, she liked the idea that the eldest grandson of Cherokee Rose Chisholm had taken notice of the only child—a daughter—of the Pruitt Ranch."

"Holy Hannah, you were only five years old."

"Which, in her mind, I think, gave me plenty of time to enthrall Sloan and make him my slave. Or some such nonsense."

Caleb's lips quirked. "Did you think it was nonsense?"

"At five I wasn't thinking in terms of slaves. I was thinking that when I grew up Sloan would marry me, and I had to do everything I could to make sure that happened."

"Good God. At the age of five?"

"What can I say? I was already programmed to become a wife and mother. Those were my goals in life. That, and being a cowgirl."

He tossed her a cocky grin. "That goes without saying."

"Thank you." She gave him a regal nod. "I guess I have my obsession with Sloan to thank for learning to be a cowgirl."

"How's that?"

"It was something Daddy picked up from Mama. She used to say things like, 'Eat your vegetables, honey, so you can grow up faster for Sloan.'"

Caleb snorted.

"Yeah, well, it worked. She would tie ribbons in my hair so I would be pretty if I saw Sloan. Everything she wanted me to do, she held out Sloan as the carrot. It got to the point where I believed I was *supposed* to eat and dress and groom and take naps to impress Sloan. Even Daddy got into the act, telling me how much more Sloan would notice me if I could rope a steer faster, saddle my own horse.''

''They brainwashed you.''

''Very effectively, but I went along with them. Eagerly, you might say, because to me he really was a hero. My hero. And when I got older and realized he was dating girls—other girls—it was okay at first, because I knew I wasn't old enough.''

''And when you were old enough?''

''He broke my heart,'' she said quietly. Calmly. She remembered the pain, but no longer felt it. ''I did everything in my power to get him to notice me, to like me the way I liked him. It never occurred to me to act any other way. Poor Sloan.''

''Poor Sloan? Why do you say that?''

''Are you kidding? All those years with me dogging his heels, showing up everyplace he went. Especially when I turned sixteen and Daddy fixed up that old pickup for me. I had wheels. I was mobile, could follow Sloan everywhere he went. God, how embarrassed he used to get.''

''He didn't want to hurt your feelings.''

''I know. I know. But the only way he could have avoided that would have been to fall madly in love with me. And I think I knew that wasn't going to happen long before I got that first set of wheels. And there you were, every time I got discouraged. You always let me cry on your shoulder, and you never tried to tell me to leave him alone, or that he would change his mind. You were just there.''

Melanie drew her horse to a halt and waited for Caleb to do the same and face her. When he did, she held his gaze steadily. ''Right where I needed you to

be. Always. Did I ever thank you for that? For a life-
time of that?''

"We were friends," he said. "Are friends. There
was never any need for thanks between you and me."

"And that," she said with a saucy grin as she
nudged Jack into motion again, "is why I love you."

At her casual, breezy words, Caleb felt a heavy
thump in his chest. He tried to laugh it off, but something was happening inside him that he didn't understand. It felt like a gathering. Knowledge. Revelation.
But it was unclear, fuzzy and just out of his reach. If
he could only stretch out his hand far enough, he might
be able to grasp it. Whatever it was.

But first he needed to catch up with the woman who
was swiftly driving him insane.

A gathering of knowledge. Ha. Nonsense was what
it was.

He caught up with her quickly, then slowed his horse
to walk beside hers. As far as he could tell, she had
yet to answer his question.

"So," he said casually, "are you saying…what are
you saying?"

"I'm saying that what I felt for Sloan was as much
habit and suggestion as it was real feelings. I didn't
just wake up one morning two years ago and decided
I didn't love him. It was more a growing feeling—no,
that's not right. Not a feeling. A slow acknowledgment
that what I felt for him was selfish and self-serving and
superficial, and Sloan and I both deserved better than
that. I decided to grow up, to give him a little peace
for a change from my constant hounding. And if I
sound as if that wasn't a painful realization, it was."

Caleb tried to filter through everything she'd said to

get to the guts of it. "Are you saying you never really, you know, loved him?"

"I sure thought I did. But now when I look back, I don't think I understood what love was. I'm not sure I know now, for that matter. But I should have wanted what was best for him, what would make him happy. But all I thought about was my feelings. That doesn't sound much like love to me."

"Come on, give yourself a break. And I doubt Sloan ever felt hounded."

"He was just too sweet to ever say so."

"Sweet?" Caleb hooted with laughter. "I've never heard anybody call him that before."

"Okay, so he was never sweet. He was always nice to me, though. He treated me just the way he thought of me. Like a kid sister. Think how much grief I could have saved us all if I'd gotten the message a few years sooner."

They rode in silence for a few minutes. Then Caleb decided to just ask outright. "So, are you really over him?"

Melanie threw her head back and laughed. "Yes, Caleb, I have been really over him for a long, long time. He's the big brother I never had."

He gave her a wry grin. "I thought that was my role."

She snorted. "Hardly. I never thought of you as a brother. You were—are—my friend. My one true friend."

Her admission both humbled and liberated him. Freed him from some nagging worry he hadn't even named. "What about Justin?"

She laughed. "Justin's my playmate." A few moments later she spoke again. "Did I tell you what you wanted to know?"

"That you're no longer hot after my brother? Yeah."

"Caleb," she said, exasperated, "I haven't been hot after Sloan for a long time and you know it. Good grief, do you think I could have hooked up with Mark Shannon last year if I still had feelings for Sloan? If I had feelings for any other man?"

Caleb stuck his tongue in his cheek. "Didn't stop you from jumping into the back seat of Tommy Newly's car your senior year of high school."

Melanie groaned and rolled her eyes. "Don't remind me. What a disaster. Are you going to hold that over my head forever?"

"I was so hacked at you over that I could have turned you over my knee."

"Ha. You could have lost a few fingers trying. I was the oldest living virgin, and it was a cinch Sloan wasn't going to do anything about it."

You could have come to me. Caleb stiffened in sheer terror that he might have spoken those words aloud. Since she didn't fall off her horse laughing, or throw her hat at him, he had to assume he'd kept his mouth shut. But the words were there, in his head. He refused to examine how long they'd been hidden in the dark recesses of his mind.

"A girl had to do something," she said with a defiant toss of her head.

"Whatever," Caleb muttered. He decided they'd had enough conversation. He wished he'd never brought up the subject of her feelings for Sloan.

They rode on in silence, and Melanie was grateful.

She had blabbered on like a fool. She was better off keeping her mouth shut.

They clambered down an embankment and up the other side of a dry wash, which put them halfway to the Angus pasture. A few minutes later Melanie's horse started favoring his right foreleg and nodding his head up and down.

"Whoa, Jack." She barely had to pull gently on the reins to have the horse stopping. "Hold up, Caleb." She swung down from the saddle and rounded to Jack's right side.

"What's wrong?"

"He's favoring this leg."

"What happened?" He dismounted and joined her.

"I don't know. He just started limping." She had checked each hoof, shoe and foot before saddling him, but she checked again, thinking maybe Jack had picked up a stone. But there was no sign of one, and the frog didn't seem to be tender when she pressed on it.

She didn't have to go far above the hoof, however, to find the problem. "Feel this." She pressed her hand over Jack's right fetlock. She checked his left ankle for comparison and found it no warmer than it should be. "His right ankle's hot."

Caleb placed his hand where she indicated and felt. "Yeah, it's hot all right."

"He must have pulled a tendon, poor boy, or bruised it on something." She stood and rubbed the horse between his ears. "Poor baby. We'll get you home and take care of you."

"Rub on some liniment or alcohol, pack a little ice around it, he'll be good as new in a few days." He rose to his feet. "We'll head back. You can ride with me."

Melanie spent another few minutes petting Jack and fretting over his leg. When Caleb remounted, Melanie handed him Jack's reins. Caleb removed his left foot from the stirrup and held an arm down for her.

Melanie gripped his forearm and he hers; she put her foot into the stirrup and, with a tug from Caleb, swung up to sit on the skirt behind the seat of the saddle. The horse moved restlessly beneath the new weight, seated farther back on his back than he cared for.

"Easy, boy," Caleb murmured. "It's just Melanie. You all set?" he asked over his shoulder.

Melanie gripped the cantle and settled her weight. "All set."

"You gonna hold on?" he asked.

"I've got a nice grip on the saddle. Take off. I'm fine."

"If you say so," Caleb muttered. He'd ridden the back end of a horse often enough to know that holding on to the saddle was no way to keep your seat unless the ground was smooth and level and you weren't in a hurry.

They weren't necessarily in a hurry today, but she was going to have a hell of a time keeping her seat without holding on to him when they climbed up out of the wash.

His horse didn't seem to care how his extra passenger held on. He wasn't pleased with the extra weight. Especially when that extra weight kept shifting and fidgeting instead of sitting still. The horse sidestepped restlessly and tossed his head.

"Easy, boy." Caleb patted the horse's neck. "What's wrong back there?" he asked Melanie over his shoulder.

"Nothing," Melanie claimed.

"Then sit still, will you, before this fellow tosses us both in the dirt."

"I know how to sit a horse, thank you."

"Then prove it." He reached around and grabbed her hand, placing it on his waist. "Hang on to me."

The minute he released her hand, she removed it from his side and shifted her weight again.

The horse gave a small buck in objection. The action threw Melanie against Caleb's back with a gasp of alarm.

Caleb swore. At the horse, at Melanie. "You all right?"

"I would be," she said, straightening away from Caleb's back, "if this ornery beast would settle down."

"He'd settle down if you'd quit moving around back there. And he's not ornery, he's uncomfortable, and not too happy about that extra weight bouncing around on his butt."

"Are you saying I weigh too much?"

"I'm saying you need to hold on to me and sit still."

He sent the horse down the incline into the dry wash.

Gravity threw Melanie forward again into Caleb's back. She tried to lean back but couldn't. And she didn't want to touch him. They had just had a long, friendly conversation, putting their friendship back on track, where it belonged. It was imperative that she not touch him, because touching him made her want to forget about friendship and move on to a more interesting relationship.

Yet if she lost his friendship, she would lose a part of herself. A vital part that she wasn't sure she wanted to live without.

As soon as they reached the bottom of the ravine she

leaned back, shifting her weight away from Caleb, and gripped the saddle again.

The horse responded with another little bump with his hindquarters, bouncing Melanie a good two inches into the air. She came down with a hard *umph*.

"Told ya," Caleb muttered.

Behind his back Melanie made a face.

"Did you just make a face at me?"

"What, have you got eyes in the back of your head now?"

"No, I just know you."

They were across the wash and starting up the other side before Melanie could psych herself up enough to voluntarily touch him again. The climb was steeper than she'd realized. Reflex and instinct, along with the fear of falling, kicked in. With a shriek she threw her arms around Caleb's waist and hung on for dear life. His warmth instantly seeped into her. The smell of her soap and his shampoo combined to tease her senses.

She wasn't sure, because of the thunder of her own pulse in her ears, but she thought she might have heard laughter. And not from the horse.

She glanced over to make sure Jack was making it okay. He seemed to be keeping up all right.

It wasn't far up the bank. The wash wasn't all that deep. They were up and over the lip in a matter of seconds. The instant the horse settled back into an easy walk Melanie shoved away from Caleb and repositioned herself.

The horse nickered, tossed his head, and kicked out with one hind leg.

"Okay, that's it." After looping the reins around the saddle horn, Caleb kicked his feet free of the stirrups, swung his right leg up and over and jumped to the ground. It wasn't an easy maneuver for a grown man who would never see thirty again, but he was just ticked enough to pull it off.

"What are you doing?" Melanie demanded.

"I'm walking," he said. "If you find touching me so distasteful that you'd rather irritate the poor damn horse to the point where he's ready to buck us both off, then I'll just walk, if it's all the same to you."

The anger in his eyes got her own dander up. She moved up into the saddle, then used the stirrup to swing down. She stood before him, her fists propped on her hips. "I just don't think it's a good idea for the two of us to get all cozy, that's all."

"Cozy?" It was almost, but not quite, a bellow.

The horses moved away to chomp the still-green grass in a less volatile atmosphere.

"You know what I'm talking about," she snapped. "Every time we get within touching distance of each other you get that look in your eyes like you're ready to lap me up, and my skin starts humming."

A quick grin curved his lips. "Humming?"

"Get over it. I'm just trying to keep things simple between us. To keep our friendship safe. All this touching and teasing and kissing is going to ruin everything." She started pacing back and forth before him, kicking at tufts of grass.

"If we keep it up," she warned, "we'll end up in bed together."

"And your problem is?"

"And if we like it enough," she said, rolling over his words, "the next thing we know, we'll be having a hot, torrid affair, then one of us will do something to hurt the other one's feelings and we'll break up, and

then not only will we not have all that great sex anymore, we won't even have our friendship.''

Caleb stared at her, dumbfounded. "All we've done
is kiss a few times and you've got us into a torrid affair,
and broken up, and not speaking to each other. Gee,
did we have any kids during all this time?"

"You are *sooo* funny."

"I'm funny? You've built this whole scenario out of
a few kisses. Do you have any idea how crazy that
sounds?"

"Of course I know how crazy it sounds," she cried,
waving her arms in the air. "And it's all your fault,
because you're making me crazy."

"*I'm* making *you* crazy?" He took his hat off and
slapped it against his leg. "What you're saying is you
want a guarantee. Like for a new car. Five years or
fifty thousand miles. Is that what you want?"

"No. Of course not."

"Well it's a damn good thing, because I'm sure as
hell no new car. For all you know, the sex will suck
for both of us, we'll have a good laugh over it and go
back to being just friends."

"Oh, yeah, right," she said. "Like it would really
suck between us."

"Yeah, I know. Not much chance of that." He
moved closer to her. "It'd be great. We both know it."

She gave a toss of her head. He doubted that her
chin could poke out any farther. "What makes you
think that?"

"This." He pulled her close and kissed her.

Somewhere in the back of her mind Melanie had
expected this. Hoped for this. Yet still he managed to
take her by surprise and lock her breath in her throat.

Along with her heart. She was helpless to do anything other than cling to him and kiss him back.

He felt hard and smooth beneath her hands as she spread them over his back. He tasted of that last cup of coffee he'd had before leaving the house.

She felt as if she'd had entirely too much coffee rather than the single cup she'd sipped. Every nerve ending danced beneath her skin.

And she wanted him. Could finally admit how much she wanted him. But she pulled back slightly and whispered, "Is this a mistake, Caleb?"

He kissed her right cheek, her left, and pulled her ball cap off, tossed it to the ground. "Do we care?" He flicked his tongue across her lips.

"No," she breathed. "No, we don't care. But in case we're wrong, let's make it a doozy." She leaned into him and ran her hands up his back and hooked them over his shoulders. She had never felt such urgency before. If she didn't get closer to him, she might die.

It was only sex. That's what she told herself. Just two willing bodies coming together to scratch an itch. It didn't have to be a big deal, and it wouldn't. It was just sex.

And it was going to be stupendous, she thought with a secret smile.

She raised one leg and rubbed it against his outer thigh, trying to get closer.

Sloan got the message and was grateful for it. He wasn't sure who took whom down, but the next thing he knew they were rolling in the grass and he had his hand on her breast. At long last. And the feel of her was infinitely better than in his dream. Softer, firmer, fuller. Real.

"I want your clothes off."

Caleb thought he'd spoken aloud what was in his mind, then realized that was Melanie's voice. He laughed, delighted. "You won't get an objection out of me."

She tugged at the snaps on his western shirt and they popped open. "Is that a fact?"

"As long as I get to return the favor."

Melanie swallowed. "Be my guest."

She was afraid to look away from his eyes, afraid she would wake up and find this was only a dream. Sunshine, the smell of autumn grass, a warm southerly breeze, and Caleb.

Don't let me wake up.

While she pulled open his shirt he worked on her buttons. But he was much too slow for her. She rose to her knees and pulled him with her, where she promptly stripped him of his shirt and took off her own.

Caleb managed, but just barely, to refrain from simply pouncing on her. She was suddenly so confident, so bold and sure of herself, so magnificent with the sunlight pouring over her pale skin, her dark hair. She took his breath away. With hands that weren't as steady as they should have been, he reached behind her and unhooked her plain white bra.

She felt the air first, then the sun on flesh that never saw the sun. Then Caleb's hands cupped her, the first man's hands to touch her this way in a long, long time. She closed her eyes and felt her breasts swell to fill his palms.

"Oh, Caleb," she whispered.

"You're beautiful," he told her.

She shook her head. "I'm not, but you make me feel that way."

"You are. Beautiful to see, to touch." He dipped his

head down and teased one nipple with his tongue. "To taste." He took the bud into his hot, wet mouth and suckled.

A deep shudder tore through her and suddenly she was on fire, burning alive from the inside out, and only Caleb could save her. She arched toward him and felt the grass cushion her back as he took her down again to the ground.

When he took his mouth away an involuntary cry of protest escaped her lips.

But he didn't leave, not really, for he kissed his way across her chest to the other nipple. It was torture of the most exquisite, most pleasurable kind.

She went wild. She had to have him inside her. Now. This instant. But there were still too damn many clothes separating them. She tried to toe off her boots, but she knew better. It took two hands or a bootjack to free her feet.

Caleb felt her struggle and chuckled against her breast. "Damn boots."

"Help me."

They rolled together, tugging and laughing and cursing the foibles of well-fitting boots. Leather flew this way and that, followed swiftly by socks. Melanie fumbled her belt buckle open and reached for her zipper.

"Wait." Caleb pressed his hand over hers. "Let me." He pushed her gently back to the grass and took his time, tugging the zipper down slowly, one notch at a time, while watching her. He was stunned, humbled, that he could bring her as much pleasure as he saw on her face.

He tugged her jeans down and off, and with them her white cotton panties. No frills for his Mel.

He hadn't known that plain, white cotton could make his heart pound like a hammer in his chest.

She squirmed on the ground, reaching for his belt buckle, but he was too busy admiring the pale length of her long, long legs to be of any help.

"So perfect," he murmured.

"Off." She freed his buckle, lowered his zipper and thrust her hands inside the back of his jeans. Her fingers dug into his flesh. The small pricks of her fingernails shot fire straight to his loins.

She was rushing him, and it was important that with her, for her, he did not rush. He knew this woman. She could face anything that came at her, except her own feelings. Hadn't she just told him that she had outgrown her feelings for Sloan years before she'd been willing to admit it?

If Caleb wanted her to have feelings for him, he was going to have to make her face them. She was going to have to face that there was more between them now than friendship. And she wouldn't want to. He had his work cut out for him. But it started here and now, on the grass in an open pasture in the sunlight. No secrets. No more hiding.

"Wait," he said. "Let me look at you."

"You can look at me with your jeans off."

"I can." He nipped at her lips. "But with my jeans off I'm more likely to do something else."

She grinned up at him. "That's the idea."

He chuckled. "Don't be in such a hurry."

She narrowed her eyes at him. "You wouldn't start something you don't intend to finish, would you?"

"Not finish? Are you out of your mind?"

She smiled again, but it was tinged with wry humor. "I'm here, aren't I?"

"Oh, that'll cost you." He buried his mouth against her neck and made growling noises.

Melanie shrieked with laughter. She'd never laughed before while having sex. Of course, they weren't exactly having sex yet, but they were getting to it. If she could just hurry Caleb along before things got too intense. She could already feel her emotions bubbling, fighting each other, trying to overtake her. Sex wasn't supposed to be so complicated. At least, it never had been for her.

This, with the laughter and the yearning in Caleb's eyes, the tenderness in his touch, was something new, something scary.

Her mind raced in a thousand directions, seeking a way to get them back on an even keel. The laughter was fine. Great in fact. But the yearning...that wouldn't do. That way lay disaster.

Then he cupped his hand between her legs and her mind blanked. What was he doing to her? Why should his touch, above any other she'd ever known, be the one to melt her bones?

She reached to push down his jeans. Caleb helped her, and as soon as he was naked she rolled him to his back and straddled his hips. "Now." She grinned down at him.

"Not yet." With a twist of his hips he had her on her back before she knew it. "Let me in, Melanie."

"Let you?" She wrapped her arms around his neck and pulled him close. "I'm about to beg you."

He traced a finger across her brow. "What are you afraid of?"

"Nothing. I'm afraid of dying before I feel you inside me."

Her admission was enough to make his blood surge.

"I want inside you. Here," he said, cupping a hand between her legs. "And here." He kissed her forehead. "And here." He kissed between her breasts, over her heart. "I want it all. Let me in, Mel, let me in."

"Caleb." She gave a frustrated groan and arched her hips against his hand.

Caleb knew what she wanted. He wanted the same thing, wanted to bury himself deep inside her and stroke until they both flew apart, together. He nudged her legs apart and settled between her thighs.

Melanie took in a breath and held it. To feel him there, between her legs, his weight covering her hips, was like nothing she'd ever known. Hot shivers raced over her skin and through her muscles. Every nerve ending in her body danced beneath her skin. But it wasn't enough. She wanted more. She wanted him.

And then he was there, easing inside her, stretching her, filling her with his hot, hard length in a way she had never before been filled. She raised her knees to take more of him.

With a groan, Caleb pushed in to the hilt. She was so tight, so hot and wet, it was all he could do to keep from pulling out and pounding into her again and again until he lost his mind, until he made her scream with pleasure.

He thought maybe he had already lost his mind, for he didn't move. "Let me in, Melanie."

Breathless, she said, "Are you kidding?"

"I don't mean just here." He nudged his hips forward. "I mean here." He kissed her forehead, and between her breasts. "And here."

Melanie arched her hips. "Caleb, please."

"Let me in."

"I don't know what you're talking about."

"Yes, you do."

"It's just sex," she said.

"It's not, and you know it." He trailed kisses across one cheek, then the other. "We mean more than that to each other. We deserve more than that from each other. Let me in."

"I don't know how," she cried in frustration, her eyes shut tight. If he didn't move soon she was going to explode.

"Just let go. Stop trying to think your way through this and just feel. Just feel, Mel."

"I can't," she cried, twisting her head away from his lips.

Caleb kissed his way down her neck, her chest, to the tip of one breast. She was so soft there, but for the hard tip. And sweet, like dark honey. "Just let go."

And she did. Something inside her, a tight control she hadn't been aware of, melted away under the heat of his mouth and in his eyes. Suddenly she was soaring.

"Caleb," she whispered in wonder.

"Look at me," he asked. "Let me see your eyes."

She opened her eyes and met his dark brown gaze.

He saw there what he'd wanted to see. A new openness, mixed with deep emotion, something more than just heat. "Oh, yeah." He took her mouth and devoured it, with lips and tongue and teeth. The need inside him burned, took over. His hands roamed everywhere, eager and greedy to feel every inch of her. His hips flexed, slowly at first, then faster and faster as she moaned and urged him on.

She took him higher than he'd ever been, meeting him thrust for thrust, gasping breath for gasping breath, pounding heartbeat for pounding heartbeat. Harder. Faster.

Melanie felt the pleasure and the pressure and the fire build until she thought she couldn't bear it, yet she never wanted it to end.

But it did, with an explosion of sensation and emotions that started low and deep, where she and Caleb were joined, and radiated out in waves, taking her with it and flinging her off the edge of the earth. She screamed in sheer release.

And then he was there with her, Caleb was with her, thrusting deep inside with a mighty groan, holding her close, keeping her safe. Sheltering her as they tumbled through space together.

The warmth of the sun on his back tempted Caleb to lie there forever. Two things kept him from giving in and falling asleep. First was that he knew his weight must be crushing Melanie. Second was the dampness on his shoulder where she pressed her face.

"Melanie?" He started to push himself up, but she clung to him with a quiet sob.

"No," she said. "Don't look at me."

"Mel…" He started to raise his hips, to pull out of her and relieve her of his weight.

"No." She tightened her legs around him. "Don't leave me. Don't leave me yet."

The words were so sweet to his ears, but for the tears in her voice. "Baby, what's wrong?"

This time she laughed. "Nothing's wrong. Nothing." Her arms squeezed more tightly around his neck. Half laughing, half crying, she gave a final squeeze then threw her arms over her head. "Nothing has ever been so right."

Caleb sagged with relief. "You had me scared. I thought… I don't know what I thought."

Inside, Melanie was shaking. Everything within her had shifted somehow, opened, leaving her feeling vulnerable to him in a new and frightening way. She couldn't let him see. She had to put some distance between them at once.

Letting out a loud sigh, she scrubbed her face dry, then slapped him on the rear. "Let me up. I've got a lame horse to get home and tend to."

Caleb rolled to her side. "I never knew you had such a romantic streak."

She let out a snort, half laughter, half disgust, and rose onto her knees to start gathering her scattered clothes. "Romantic, hell. What's the big deal? It was just sex."

"The hell it was." He took her arm and pulled her around to face him. "It was more than that, and you know it."

Melanie shivered. There was more than anger in his eyes. Mere anger she could deal with. But hurt looked out at her from those brown depths. Hurt she had caused.

She felt small and mean. After what the two of them had just shared, there should have been soft words and lingering glances. But the fear in her was bigger than her conscience or her need for reassurance from her lover. Or his need for something from her.

"Okay," she said, pulling her arm free and picking up her underwear from the grass. "It was really great sex."

He yanked her panties from her grasp. "What are you afraid of?"

"Right now?" She grabbed up her jeans and tugged them on. "Sunburn. I said it was great sex. So great, in fact," she added, picking up her bra and putting it on, "that after we get back and I take care of Jack, we can do it again, if you want."

Her casual crude remark left Caleb speechless, but not for long. "I don't believe you."

"I'm sorry." She whipped her shirt on, then sat down to put on her socks and boots, all the time refusing to meet his gaze. "I didn't mean to hurt your feelings. I told you this was a bad idea."

Caleb didn't trust himself to speak, for fear he would say something he wouldn't be able to take back. His best friend, the woman he had just taken as his lover, was lying through her pearly-white teeth. She must be badly shaken to be pulling a stunt like this.

Tight-lipped, he gathered up his own clothes. "If you're in a hurry, don't wait on me. I can walk back."

"Don't be silly. It was my horse that went lame. I'll walk. It'll only take about ten minutes."

"Oh, yeah, right." He put on his socks first, then tugged on his jeans while she put on her boots. "Like I'm gonna ride off and leave you afoot."

"I don't know why not." She stood up and stomped her feet more firmly into her boots. "I would you."

"We've already covered what a lousy liar you are, more than once lately, so give it a rest, will you?"

"Jack and I are walking back," she said. "If you and Blazer want to walk with us, that's fine."

Melanie had been accurate about it taking only ten minutes to walk back to the house, out of sight until they topped the rise. Back at the barn, Caleb tied Blazer's reins to the corral fence.

"You want me to saddle you another horse? We've still got time to bring the herd up here before dark."

Melanie squinted up at the sun to judge the time for

herself. It was nearly noon. She shook her head. "I'm hungry. I'll decide after lunch. Go ahead and turn Blazer out in the corral for now."

"Yes, ma'am."

Melanie eyed him carefully. Dammit, she'd known if they took their kissing any further they would gum up the works. *Yes, ma'am,* she mimicked silently. "What's that supposed to mean?"

"Nothing." He untied Blazer's reins and led him toward the barn to unsaddle him. "Nothing at all. You're the one calling all the shots."

"That's right," she said. "I am."

"Yes, ma'am." He took his horse into the barn.

Melanie followed with Jack and they unsaddled their mounts. Caleb rubbed down his horse while Melanie got the liniment from the tack room and spent nearly ten minutes rubbing it into Jack's fetlock. Then she led him outside where she turned on the hose and ran cold water over the injury for another ten minutes.

"There, Jack, that will help, I promise. And we'll do it again in a little while." She would repeat the process three or four times a day for as long as three days if need be. If he wasn't recovered by then she would have to talk to the vet about anti-inflammatory drugs.

Meanwhile, to help things along she went to the house and filled a large Ziploc bag with crushed ice. She took this out to the barn and tied it around Jack's ankle. He probably wouldn't leave it in place very long, but every minute it stayed on would help.

With the ice pack firmly in place, she gave him a rubdown and a handful of sweet feed.

By the time she and Caleb both finished, they had

shared fewer than a dozen words, and each of them only out of necessity. And each one bitten off tersely.

When they finished, she turned toward the big barn doors. "If you want to eat, come to the house."

Caleb would have told her to take her offer of food and shove it, but the cell phone clipped to his belt chose that moment to chirp.

One of them had just been saved, he thought, by the bell.

He unclipped the phone and answered. It was Justin.

"You coming home anytime soon?" Justin demanded. "Work's piling up around here."

"Work's always piling up," Caleb said easily. "What's new since last night when Sloan told me everything was fine?"

"Cal just called. He'll be here in an hour."

Cal was their cousin from Georgia. "With the mare?"

"You got it. You coming?"

Caleb watched Melanie march stiff-backed toward the house. Stomped was more like it. A little more distance between the two of them seemed like a good idea just then. Besides, Cal was bringing in the new mare Sloan had been wanting. Big brother didn't know it yet, but Caleb and Justin had gone together and bought her for him as a wedding present. They'd hoped to have her home in time to present her to Sloan and Emily at the party last Saturday, but that hadn't been possible. Now that she was finally coming, Caleb had to be on hand.

"Yeah," he told Justin. "I'll be there in twenty."

He ended the call, reclipped the phone onto his belt and caught up with Melanie in the kitchen.

"I've got to run home for a couple of hours," he said.

"Fine. You don't need to come back. I'm sure Daddy will be home this evening."

Caleb ground his teeth together. "Are you deliberately trying to hack me off, or does it just come naturally?"

She raised her eyebrows. "I don't know what you're talking about."

Caleb stared at her and shook his head slowly. "We're not finished with this."

"Oh, I think we are."

"Not by a long shot, pal. I'll be back. Count on it. Meanwhile, do us both a favor and stick close to the house in case you get any more unwanted visitors."

She smirked. "Are you kidding? I'm about to get rid of one."

"Look." He jabbed a finger toward her face. "I don't know what's eating you, but we're going to have this out when I get back."

He didn't give her a chance to answer. He grabbed his wallet and keys from the counter, then spun on his heel and strode swiftly outside to his pickup. When he climbed into the seat he tossed his wallet down beside him.

His wallet. Where he kept his driver's license, credit card, voter's registration. And the condom he always carried, just in case.

Well, hell.

Chapter Six

The minute Caleb drove across the cattle guard at the end of the PR drive—and Melanie knew when that minute came because she rushed to the front door and watched him drive away—she went to the kitchen sink to scrub away the stink of horse liniment. By the time she finished, her skin was raw. But the smell of liniment was gone.

The smell of Caleb, however, was another matter. He was on her skin, on her clothes, in her hair.

Oh, God, what had she done?

The tears came from nowhere, shocking her with their intensity. She *hated* crying, and here she was, for the second time in one day, sobbing her eyes out. Dammit.

But she couldn't seem to stop. She wrapped her arms around her middle, for comfort, she supposed, and

leaned over the sink, her tears so thick they blocked
her vision.

He had overwhelmed her, made her open herself up
to him, open her heart to him the way she never had
before, not for any man. Not even for herself. And it
hurt.

But she had hurt him, too, and she hadn't known she
could, not over plain, ordinary sex. Not even over spec-
tacular sex. They were friends. They should not have
been able to breach each other's internal barriers.

And dammit, she thought with a sniff, she should
not still be crying. Crying solved nothing; all it did was
stop up her nose and turn her face red and splotchy.

After a few more sniffs she turned on the faucet and
splashed cold water on her face. Jack had probably torn
off his ice pack by now. She took a stack of gel cold
packs from the pantry and put them in the freezer for
use later, then went back out to the barn to see about
her horse.

At the Cherokee Rose, Caleb parked beside the barn
where Justin and Sloan stood waiting for him.

"About damn time you decided to put in an appearance," Sloan said tersely.

"If you needed me," Caleb said calmly, "you knew
where I was."

"I knew." Sloan eyed him carefully. "What I want
to know is why. What are you up to with Melanie?"

Justin elbowed his way between them and faced
Caleb. "Are you taking advantage of her?"

"Oh, yeah, that's right, jump on me. Get your minds
out of the gutter, both of you." Never mind that his
own had been there for the better part of the week. "It

so happens she's all alone out there on the PR with no one to help her. I've been giving her a hand.''

"What do you mean, alone?" Sloan demanded. "Where's her dad, where are their men?"

"They're having trouble. Her dad's gambling again and they had to let the men go. And that's probably not for public consumption."

"Why the hell didn't she say something sooner?" Justin demanded.

"Why the hell didn't any of us notice sooner?" Sloan asked with disgust.

"Well, it's done." Caleb shifted. He thought he heard the rumble of a truck engine approaching. "I'm helping out, and when Ralph Pruitt shows his face again I intend to straighten him out, one way or another."

Justin gave a sharp tug on the brim of his hat. "You need any help in that department, I'll be more than happy to lend a hand. He's got no business leaving her with all that work and responsibility. But right now, we've got something else to do."

"Who's this?" Sloan motioned toward the pickup and horse trailer coming up the driveway. "Somebody must be lost."

Caleb and Justin shared a grin.

"Not exactly," Justin said. "I'll go get Emily and Grandmother. They'll want to see this."

"See what?" Sloan demanded as Justin ran off toward the house. "Hey, that looks like…is that Cal? What's he doing here?"

Caleb kept quiet until the others arrived and Cal stepped out of the pickup.

"Hey, guys."

"Cal?" Sloan strode forward to shake hands with

their cousin. "What the hell are you doing here? How long can you stay?"

"Save your questions, big guy." Justin slapped Sloan on the back. "Let's unload that trailer first."

When Sloan saw the horse in the trailer, he didn't have to be told who it was. He recognized the mare he'd fallen in love with last year in Kentucky.

"Cherokee Beauty," he breathed. "Where are you taking her?" he asked Cal.

"Here," Cal said.

"Here? What do you mean, here?"

Caleb and Justin shared a look, then laughed. "Happy wedding," Caleb said, putting a hand on Sloan's shoulder.

Sloan blinked. "What?"

"You heard me. She's yours. Yours and Emily's. A belated wedding present."

Sloan appeared stunned. "Man. She's ours? No fooling?"

It wasn't often that Sloan Chisholm was taken by surprise. Caleb was pleased and proud to have been in on the surprise that so obviously held his brother in awe.

In Caleb's book, Sloan was the best. He worked like a dog to make sure everyone he loved was taken care of. It felt good, damn good, to be able to do something good for him for a change.

Having just washed another application of liniment off, Melanie was standing with her back to the kitchen window, drying her hands, when she heard a vehicle drive up to the back of the house.

She groaned. She wasn't ready to face Caleb yet.

Outside, a car door slammed.

Melanie threw her towel onto the counter. Ready or not, her time seemed to have run out. She turned toward the back door just as it flew open.

"I'm home!"

Melanie gaped. It took her a moment to fight her way through the shock, the relief, to find her voice. "Mama!"

"Baby!" Fayrene Pruitt swept her daughter up in a tight hug.

Melanie hugged her back, fiercely glad to see for herself that her mother was all right. In the brief glimpse she'd had before her mother reached her, Melanie had noted that even discounting the cosmetics, her mother's color was good, her eyes clear and filled with delight.

Mama was okay. Thank God, Mama was okay, and she was home.

But as she stood there in her mother's beloved arms Melanie became aware that something was different. Her mother had finally lost the extra weight she'd been threatening to shed for years. Melanie pushed back and grinned.

"Mama, you're all skinny." At least compared to her former shape. Fayrene had always been a little on the pudgy side. Now she was trim and curvy.

Fayrene grinned. "Well, not all of me." She wagged her shoulders forward and back.

"Mama, you look great. You're—" Then Melanie saw what was truly different about her mother's shape, and she gaped. Her eyes felt ready to pop clear out of her head. "Mama! What have you done?"

Where once a nice, comfortable set of A-cup breasts had rested reliably, there now sat perched the grandest pair of D-cups Melanie had ever seen.

"Mama!"

Fayrene threw back her head and laughed. "You like 'em?"

"What have you done?"

Fayrene held her arms in the air and danced around in a circle. She wore blue jeans that looked painted on, a silver concho belt and a red, Western style blouse with white piping and, along the yoke, fringe, which only accented her new breasts.

"*This* is what you had done at the Scottsdale Clinic?"

Fayrene patted her new breasts. "They did a really nice job, too."

All the worry, all the fear for her mother's life, and she'd had a boob job? Melanie didn't know whether to laugh, cry or throttle her mother.

She did all three. She started laughing, hysterically, then went for her mother's throat. "I could strangle you." Tears came through the laughter. "I thought you were sick or dying. Dammit, Mama, you scared the daylights out of me."

Fayrene stepped back and gaped. "Why on earth would you think something like that?"

"What am I supposed to think when you charge ten thousand dollars on the credit card at a place called Scottsdale Clinic? And then you don't return my phone calls? And while we're on the subject, how in the *hell* are we supposed to pay that bill?"

Fayrene's mouth opened and closed like a fish sucking air. "What do you mean?" she finally managed to say.

"Hell-o-o." Melanie tapped a finger against her mother's temple. "When you charge on the credit card,

I have to come up with the cash to pay the credit card company.''

Fayrene shook her finger in Melanie's face. ''Don't you talk to me that way, young lady. I'm still your mother.''

''I know you are, and I love you, and I respect you. But between you and Daddy—''

''What about your daddy?''

Melanie shook her head and turned away. ''He's—'' She paused at the sound of another vehicle approaching the house. She glanced out the window.

''He's what, baby?''

''He's here,'' Melanie said. ''He just pulled up.'' A man was in the pickup with him, and another man followed in a sedan.

Just great, Melanie thought. What a time for her dad to bring company home with him.

If she had been counting to ten she wouldn't have finished before her father burst through the back door. ''Mel?'' Then he saw his wife. His eyes popped. ''Good grief! Fayrene? Holy smokes! What the hell have you done to yourself?''

''Well,'' Fayrene said, propping her hands on her hips and thrusting out her new, more-than-ample chest, ''it looks like I finally have your attention. For once.''

''What the hell is that supposed to mean?'' Ralph demanded.

''Wait a minute,'' Melanie said, stunned. ''You don't mean to tell me that you did this just to get Daddy's attention.''

''It worked, didn't it?'' Fayrene smirked. ''Look at him. He can't take his eyes off me.''

''He's staring at your boobs.''

''Yes.'' Fayrene's smile was pure feline. ''He is.''

"I am not." Ralph jerked his gaze away from his wife's chest for the first time since entering the house. "Okay, I was," he grumbled. "Hell's bells, look at 'em? Who wouldn't stare?"

"Daddy, for heaven's sake."

"No, baby," Fayrene said. "It's quite all right. This is exactly how I'd hoped he'd react."

"Good God, you *did* do it for him," Melanie cried.

"Of course. Why else would a woman do such a thing?"

Melanie groaned in frustration. She and her mother had entirely different personalities and ways of thinking. Thank goodness.

Outside the back door the man who had ridden with her father started whistling.

Melanie's father jumped as if jabbed by a cattle prod. "A couple of guys came with me."

"I can see that," Melanie said. "Who are they? Why are they here?"

"I made a deal."

"You've been gambling again," Fayrene accused.

Ralph glared at Melanie.

"Don't look at me," she declared. "I didn't say a word."

Fayrene huffed. "She didn't have to. You look guilty as hell, the place looks run-down and our baby girl is griping about money. If that isn't enough, I recognize a couple of goons when I see them," she added, nodding toward the two men outside. "What have you got yourself into this time, Ralphie?"

Ralph pulled a handkerchief from his back pocket and wiped it across his forehead. "Look, you two. I owe these guys' boss a lot of money, money Melanie says we don't have. I made a deal with him to clear my slate, but you can't talk about it, either of you, to anyone. Not ever, do you hear me? Not ever."

Melanie had never seen her father so distraught. He looked as if he might throw up any minute. "Let's sit at the table and have some iced tea while you tell us about it," she suggested.

Ralph seized the idea like a lifeline. However, he wasn't so distracted by his problems that he didn't have the presence of mind to pull out the chair at the foot of the table for her mother before seating himself at the head of the table.

"I can't believe you're here," Ralph said to his wife as Melanie filled glasses with ice.

"I can't believe you've been gambling," Fayrene said softly.

While Melanie poured tea, her father stared down at his folded hands and blushed.

Good for you, Mama, Melanie thought. Maybe her mother could reach Daddy, when Melanie had been unable to.

"Okay," Melanie said, giving them their glasses and taking a seat between them. "What's this deal you made?"

Ralph stalled by taking a long, deep gulp of tea. Finally he put the glass down and swallowed. "I made a deal with Bruno."

"Oh, God," Fayrene cried. "You owe money to somebody named Bruno? I suppose his last name is Corleone or Gotti or something."

Ralph rolled his eyes. "His last name, Miss Smarty-Pants, is McGuire. Bruno McGuire. Now just hush up, both of you, and let me tell this. Sometime late tonight somebody's going to drive a pickup or truck or something in and park it in the pasture behind the barn. A little while after that, Bruno and some of his people will come, split up the cargo and leave. In a couple of weeks they'll do it all again, and my debt will be wiped out.''

Melanie did not like the sound of this. ''What kind of cargo has to be driven in and split up in the middle of a pasture, in the middle of the night?''

''I don't know,'' her father said. ''I didn't ask, and you won't, either. We don't need to know. All we need to do is stay in the house until it's all over with.''

''What kind of trouble are you getting us into with this deal?'' she demanded.

''I'm keeping my kneecaps whole,'' he barked back. ''Don't give me any grief on this, little girl. Just keep quiet and go along with it.''

''What are the two goons outside for?'' she demanded, far from satisfied with his response.

Ralph shifted in his chair and looked decidedly uncomfortable. ''George is going to wait here so he can call Bruno when the shipment arrives.''

''What about the other one?''

Ralph flushed. ''That's Little Donnie.''

Melanie leaned sideways to look out the door at the two-hundred-fifty-pound ball of lard leaning against the front fender of his sedan. ''*Little* Donnie?''

''Yeah, well. He's gonna park out across the driveway and make sure nobody drives in except the truck they're expecting.''

''Oh, that's great.'' Melanie slapped her palms onto the table. ''That's just great. In other words, we're prisoners here. In our own house.''

''Now, little girl, don't—''

George tapped on the back door. ''Hi, folks. Mind

if I come in?'' Without waiting for an answer, he pulled open the storm door and let himself in.

Melanie glared at her father. Anger didn't come close to defining the fury she felt at his bringing these goons into their home. Neither did terror. For all she knew, these guys were here to kill them once they got what they wanted from them.

The first problem arose when Melanie announced she was going to the barn to give Jack's ankle another treatment.

George had other ideas. ''Sorry, miss, but you'll want to stay in the house for the rest of the day.''

''Look—George, is it?''

''That's right.'' The man grinned like an idiot.

He might very well be an idiot, Melanie thought, but he had mean eyes. And a windbreaker. Gray slacks and blue shirt, and a navy blue windbreaker. On television, the only reason a guy wore a windbreaker when it was warm enough to do without one was to hide a gun.

She shook her head, certain she was being ridiculous. Even if he did have mean eyes.

''Well, look, George,'' she said. ''I've got a lame horse out there who needs care. If I don't get out there and tend to him once more today, then three times again tomorrow, he could become permanently lame. Since none of us wants that to happen, I'll just go take care of him and be back in a half hour or so.''

George motioned to her parents. ''Then we'll all go with you.''

Melanie glanced down at the man's shiny, black patent-leather shoes and smirked. ''Suit yourself.'' She'd have to be sure and find a nice fresh pile of manure for him to step in. Too bad there weren't any cattle at the barn. A juicy cow patty would be just the thing.

George proved adept at stepping around the horse droppings in the barn, but there was nothing he could do to avoid the bits of straw and alfalfa that floated through the air and clung to his once-clean slacks.

And Melanie made sure to splatter a little water on his patent leathers.

She started to give him a nice dousing with liniment, but decided against it when she realized she might very well be stuck in the same house with him for hours.

She would like to send him packing. Getting herself and her parents into the house and locking George out would be simple enough. But her father had asked her to behave. He wanted to do this deal to wipe out his debt. Since she was the one who had cut off his cash, rendering him unable to pay up, she owed him her cooperation. And her loyalty.

Back in the house Melanie scrubbed liniment from her hands for the third time that day.

"You did good with Jack," her father told her. "It's not a bad sprain. He'll be good as new in another day or two."

"You think so?" No one knew more about taking care of animals than her father.

"Yep."

The phone rang. Ralph picked it up. "Caleb. Howdy. Sure, she's here. Hold on." He held the phone out toward Melanie. "It's Caleb, for you."

The sound of his name. That was all it took to make her pulse flutter in her throat. "I'll, uh, take it in my bedroom."

After she picked up the extension in her room and

her father had hung up the one in the kitchen, she closed her bedroom door.

"Your dad came back," Caleb said.

"That's not even the half of it." She forgot, for a moment, that she was angry with him and the reason for it. Instead she remembered only their friendship, the safety and security she felt in being able to tell him anything and know he would never judge her. "Mama came home today, too."

"She's all right?"

Melanie chuckled. "Well, she's healthy."

"You must be relieved."

"I would be more relieved if Daddy hadn't brought two creeps home with him."

"You're kidding."

"I wish. I—"

Her bedroom door flew open.

"What do you think you're doing?" she demanded harshly.

"You need to come out here with the rest of us."

"Listen, you creep." Oh, this man had way overstepped. "You get out of here right this minute and I won't rip out your tongue. But you so much as look at my bedroom again and I'll peel the hide off your face with my teeth."

On the other end of the phone line Caleb stiffened. One of her father's goons was in her bedroom?

"Melanie?" he said. When she didn't answer, he repeated himself, louder.

All he heard was her sharp "Get out." Then, incredibly, the line went dead.

Alarmed, Caleb hung up and redialed. The phone rang a dozen times without an answer.

Maybe he had misdialed. He tried again, his palms starting to sweat. He didn't like this. Not one damn bit.

Still no answer.

"That cuts it," he muttered. He grabbed his hat and started out the front door. "Something's going on over at the PR. I'm headed over there."

Melanie gaped, outraged. George had not only unplugged her bedroom extension from the wall, but he'd surprised her with a hard yank that jerked the phone from her hand.

"Hey!"

Before she realized what he was doing, he'd rushed through every room in the house—there weren't that many of them—and gathered up all the phones. There weren't that many of those, either; Melanie's room, the kitchen and one on the desk in the den. He put them in a pile on the floor next to the sofa and announced there would be no more calls in or out, without his approval.

"Did you agree to this?" Melanie hissed at her father.

Ralph flushed and looked away. "Just go along with it. It's only for this one night."

"And another in a couple of weeks. What about the time in between? They're going to trust us all that time, but not tonight?"

Her father opened his mouth, then shut it and shook his head, saying nothing.

Caleb broke every posted speed limit between the Cherokee Rose and the Pruitt Ranch. On the way he tried twice more to call her from his cell phone. There was still no answer. In frustration he tossed the phone onto the seat beside him and gripped the steering wheel.

He barreled up the PR's gravel driveway and had to slam on the breaks when a brown sedan pulled out from the yard and blocked his way.

What the hell?

A short, round man—really round, Caleb thought—climbed laboriously from the car and waddled over to the pickup.

Melanie had said her dad had brought home two creeps. One was, or had been, in the house. Was this creep number two?

"Hi there," the man said.

"Afternoon," Caleb offered, barely refraining from swearing. "Mind moving your car?"

When the fat man chuckled, everything on him from cheeks to belly quivered. "I'm afraid I can't do that. The family's having a private evening together. They're not accepting visitors just now. You'll need to come back tomorrow."

"Not accepting—no, never mind. I have business with them that can't wait. I'm asking you, politely, to move your car."

The man's eyes narrowed, and Caleb saw the hard meanness in them. "And I'm telling you, politely, you'll have to leave."

Caleb glanced toward the house, tapped his fingers on the steering wheel. "I guess we're through being polite. Tell you what. You move your car and you can keep that nice pretty paint job. Because I'll tell you, I'm going up to the house, whether you move your car or not."

"Whoa, now," the man said jovially. "No need to make threats, mister."

"Threats?" Caleb bared his teeth in a parody of a smile. "That wasn't a threat, that was a fact." Without giving the man time for a reaction, Caleb spun his steering wheel to the right and pressed the gas pedal. There was almost enough room between the front bumper of the sedan and the barbed-wire fence a few feet beyond the driveway.

Caleb would be damned before he would take out a neighbor's fence. His pickup could be repaired. He didn't much care what happened to the sedan. He drove through. The force of the sturdy pickup shoved the sedan aside with an audible crunch and screech of metal on metal.

The fat man bellowed in outrage.

Caleb ground his teeth and slung gravel all the way to the back door of the house. Ralph Pruitt's pickup was there, along with a car with Arizona plates. Fayrene's, he assumed.

The fat guy was huffing and puffing his way after him, waving his arms and hollering.

Caleb got out of the pickup and strode purposely to the back door, intent on getting to Melanie as fast as he could. The door opened before he could reach for the knob.

The first thing he saw was the gun.

Chapter Seven

When Melanie saw Caleb walk through the door, urged along by George's gun, her breath caught. She wished, desperately for his sake, that he had stayed home. She was chagrined, maybe even a little ashamed, to admit to herself how glad she was that he hadn't. Just having him in the same room steadied her, made her feel safer, more secure.

In that moment when their eyes met and she read his concern for her, she forgot that she wanted him at arm's length. She wanted him close. Wanted his arms around her.

But that couldn't be. Not here, not now, not in front of her parents and the creep named George.

In all honesty, even if she and Caleb were alone—especially if they were alone—she wouldn't let him get close enough to put his arms around her.

* * *

Caleb stood in the familiar kitchen where he'd had breakfast that very morning and silently cursed himself. Damn his hide. He'd known there was trouble at the PR, yet he'd been stupid enough to leave his pistol and his cell phone in the pickup and walk right into a trap.

The man with the gun was tall and lean, with olive skin and dark eyes that held that same mean look as the fat man's had.

Caleb took a step forward and stopped. "Mrs. Pruitt, it's good to..." Mercy sakes, she sure looked...different. Even with a gun on him he had to struggle to keep from staring at her chest. "...see you." He gave her a nod. "Mr. Pruitt." He nodded at Melanie's father. "Melanie." He nodded to her, too. "Is everybody all right?"

"We're fine," Melanie said.

Caleb eyed her. "I knew you were mad when I left earlier, but I didn't think you were this mad." He cut his gaze toward the gun still pointing in his direction.

Ralph Pruitt cleared his throat. "George, Bruno didn't say anything about guns."

"Let's all go into the living room," George said, "and have a seat."

Caleb gave serious thought to tackling the man. If it had been just the two of them he might have done it. But that gun could easily go off. Melanie or one of her parents could get hurt.

He went to the living room with the others, as ordered. The first thing he noticed was the pile of telephones beside the sofa.

"All we have to do," George told them, "is watch a little television and behave ourselves. Ralph's new business partner has a little business to transact later on tonight. Little Donnie and I are just here to make sure nobody gets in the way and gets hurt. See? Simple. Now, sit.''

And so they sat. Ralph, Fayrene and George took the sofa, leaving the recliner and wingback for Melanie and Caleb.

"I told you not to come back," Melanie muttered.

"What do you think of my new shape, Caleb?" Fayrene asked.

Melanie choked.

Ralph made a funny squealing sound.

George hooted.

Caleb chuckled and winked. "Looking good, Mrs. P. Real good. New hairdo?"

"Ha!" Fayrene laughed hysterically and slapped her knee.

Ralph scowled. "You blind, boy?"

"New hairdo," Fayrene shrieked. "That's a good one, Caleb."

"Good grief." Melanie snatched the remote control from the coffee table. "Give me that." She called up the satellite-TV on-screen program guide to look for something to watch. There wasn't a person in the room she was currently interested in talking to. They were all lunatics.

"I don't suppose anyone wants to tell me what this is all about," Caleb said.

"The less you know," George told him, "the better off you are."

"Now why," Caleb said lazily, "did I know you were going to say that?"

After a long silence, during which everyone looked at everyone else, looked everywhere but at the gun in George's hand, Ralph finally cleared his throat.

"What brought you here, Caleb?" he asked.

Caleb glanced to Melanie, but her expression was closed to him. Caleb shrugged. "I was on the phone with Melanie and we got cut off. I tried calling back several times, but got no answer. I was concerned."

Ralph nodded and looked down at his hands. "It's good of you to come all the way over here to check on us."

"You should know," Caleb said with another glance at Melanie, "that except for a couple of hours today, I've been here since Monday night."

Ralph bobbed his head another couple of times, then snapped to attention, his eyes going wide. "Here?" he demanded. "Since Monday?"

"That's right."

George hooted again. "This is getting good. What happened?"

Melanie's expression wasn't closed now, it was disgusted.

"Alone?" Fayrene asked carefully. With a hint of craftiness that made Caleb wince. "You and Melanie have been here alone, together, since Monday?"

Caleb leaned forward and rested his elbows on his knees. "That's right."

"Caleb." Melanie's voice was almost a wail. She flopped back in her chair and threw an arm over her eyes.

"This is better than a soap opera," George offered with an eager grin.

Melanie lowered her arm and snarled. "Shut up, George."

"Well, well." Fayrene arched an eyebrow. Speculation danced in her eyes as she glanced from Caleb to Melanie and back again. Then she jabbed an elbow into her husband's side. "Where have you been since Monday?"

"I had business," Ralph said defensively.

"So you went off and left our daughter alone with Caleb?"

"I didn't know Caleb was here."

"No," Caleb agreed. "But you knew you were leaving her here to do the work of three or four men."

Ralph gnawed on the inside of his jaw and eyed Caleb. "Did you get the hay in?"

"Daddy!" Melanie cried, outraged. "You ought to be apologizing for putting a neighbor to this much trouble, not asking how much work he got done."

"We got the hay in," Caleb said. "And the fence repaired. Oh, and we put a gate in between the PR and the Rose down in the middle of one of your pastures."

Ralph blinked. He looked as if he was having trouble taking everything in. Caleb couldn't say he blamed the man. A bookie's goons bringing him home for some kind of shady business to keep his kneecaps whole, his wife showing up with a new...shape. His neighbor moving in with his daughter and making decisions regarding his ranch.

In the same place, Caleb would be having a little trouble taking it all in, too.

About an hour after dark George had to go to the bathroom. Because he would not leave the others alone, he took Ralph with him.

"If anybody's missing when we come back," George warned, "well, it wouldn't go too good for poor Ralph, here, if you get my meaning. And no phone calls," he added.

The instant the bathroom door closed, Caleb pounced. "What the hell is going on?"

Melanie dropped her head against the back of the chair. God, how much humiliation could one woman be expected to stand? With her eyes closed, she told Caleb what was happening.

"It looks like you were more right than you knew," she told him, "when you called them goons."

"So we're just going to sit around and let this joker hold a gun on us all night?" he asked.

"You have a better idea? One that doesn't get any of us hurt?"

"It wouldn't be hard to—"

"And gets Daddy out of debt?"

"Oh, well, if you're gonna get picky."

"I'll tell you what I'd like to do," Fayrene said in a heated whisper. "I'd like to shoot that George character right between the eyes for threatening Ralphie, for making him let them do whatever it is they're doing out there in the pasture tonight. And I'd do it, too, put a bullet between his eyes, but he's got the key to the gun cabinet."

"Mama, I don't want to hear any more talk about shooting."

Fayrene huffed and folded her arms beneath her breasts, making them look even larger.

Melanie dared a glance at Caleb and found him staring somewhere in the vicinity of the top of her mother's head. Bless his heart, he was working diligently to avoid offending anyone by staring at her mother's chest. Melanie, unable to avoid staring herself—it was, after all, quite a sight—had to admire his tact and control.

Maybe in about ten years she might get used to her mother's new look. Maybe.

"We'll just have to grit our teeth and wait this out," Melanie said.

Caleb hoped it would be that simple, but he had his doubts. Why would George and his pals want to leave a bunch of witnesses who could identify at least two of them?

On the other hand, if things went according to plan, the only charge that would stick would be home invasion, if that was a legitimate charge, because Caleb and the others would never get near this so-called merchandise and wouldn't know what it was. The only evidence would be tire tracks in the pasture.

So they seemed to be more or less stuck here, waiting it out, then letting the bastards go. Hoping the bastards would let them go.

He turned the situation over in his mind and thought maybe it wouldn't be in this Bruno character's best interests to leave a bunch of dead bodies around. He was obviously, in addition to whatever this business tonight meant, a bookie. How could he make any more money off Ralph if he killed him?

Then, too, if George was bent on killing them, why hadn't he already done it?

One thing was certain. If they all got out of this alive, Caleb was going to butt his nose in and have a serious talk with Ralph. The man had no right to endanger his wife and daughter this way. Granted, he probably hadn't know Fayrene was here, but he had deliberately brought George into Melanie's home. Whatever Caleb had to do to see that such a thing never happened again, including tying Ralph up and tossing him in a closet, he would do.

* * *

The hours of the evening and night crawled by at a snail's pace. It was just after one in the morning when two pairs of headlights cut across the backyard.

Ralph jumped to his feet. "Is that them?"

George waved him back. "Stay there. I'll check on it."

But when George moved to the kitchen, everyone got up and followed him. George opened the back door and looked out. Ralph and Fayrene followed him, while Melanie went to the window over the kitchen sink.

Caleb stood at her back and looked out over her head. He placed a hand on her shoulder for the simple reason that he couldn't go another single minute without touching her.

When she raised her hand toward his, he knew she was going to push his hand away. But she didn't. Instead she stroked his fingers, sending hot shivers up his arm. Then, with her back still turned toward him as she watched out the window, she threaded her fingers through his and squeezed.

Outside, a two-toned pickup with a white camper shell covering the bed drove beneath the utility light, then past the barn and on toward the pasture over the rise, down near the spot where Melanie and Caleb had made love that day. A small, light-colored car followed.

Out at the edge of the yard, near the mouth of the driveway, Little Donnie waved his flashlight. To signal back, George flipped the porch light on and off.

Several minutes later the small car came back from the pasture. As it passed beneath the utility light, two people were plainly visible where there had been only one before.

The car stopped for the driver to speak to Little Donnie, then drove away.

"Now what?" Melanie wondered aloud.

George shooed her parents back inside the house and pulled a cell phone from his pocket. He pressed a couple of buttons and put the phone to his ear.

"It's George," he said. "The truck's here, and Hank's bringing the driver to you right now. Yeah, everything's fine here. The daughter's boyfriend showed up, but he's behaving himself. Okay, boss, we'll see you when you get here."

George ended the call and slipped the cell phone back into his pocket.

"Now what?" Melanie asked again.

"Now we wait."

"We've been waiting," she said tartly.

"And the first part is over. The goods have arrived. As soon as the driver checks in with Bruno, Bruno and some of the guys will come down and divvy up the goods, then we'll all go home and you good people can have your lives back."

"Wouldn't that be nice," Melanie muttered. "How long might this next part take?"

George shoved the back door shut and locked it. "It'll take as long as it takes. Might as well make yourselves comfortable. In the living room, if you please."

Fayrene heaved a huge sigh, which made her chest rise to impressive levels. George nearly drooled.

"Well," Fayrene said. "If we're going to be up and awake, we might as well have some coffee. Is it all right if I make coffee?" She smiled coyly at George.

Ralph pulled his gaze away from his wife's breasts long enough to scowl at her.

"Sure thing, Mrs. Pruitt. I'd like some coffee."

"Fine, then." Fayrene all but batted her lashes at him. "You all just go right on and make yourselves comfortable. I'll start the coffee."

"All right, everybody, let's go have a seat," George said.

"I'll stay and help Mama," Melanie said, turning toward the coffeemaker on the counter without giving him a chance to object.

When the others had gone to the living room Melanie hissed at her mother, "What are you doing, playing up to that creep?"

"Just watch your mother, baby, and learn a thing or two."

"What are you up to?" Melanie whispered.

"Shh. Get me a filter. Where's the coffee? You've moved it."

Together they managed to take twice as long to start the coffee brewing as Melanie would have alone. But it was so good to have her mother home that Melanie didn't mind the added confusion in the least.

Melanie stared as the coffeemaker sent hot water streaming through the coffee in the filtered basket and out into the carafe. "We've missed you, Mama. Both of us."

Fayrene stood next to her daughter and stared at the same sight. "I've missed you. Both of you. I'm sorry about the money I've been spending. I didn't realize…"

Melanie frowned and looked at her mother. "How could you not realize? We've never had the kind of money you've been spending."

Fayrene heaved a sigh. "Okay, I guess I knew that. I don't think I cared. All I ever wanted was his attention, you know?"

"Oh, Mama." Melanie wrapped an arm around her mother's shoulders and laid her head on her shoulder. "He loves you. He's been so lonely without you. I wish…"

"I know, baby, I know. I wish it, too. But don't give up on us yet. I haven't. So, what's this I hear about Sloan getting married?"

Melanie straightened away from her mother. "He got married last summer. Where did you hear it?"

"I have my ways. What I want to know is why you didn't tell me yourself."

Melanie gave her mother a wry smile and took the sugar bowl from the cabinet. "Because I didn't want to hear what you'd have to say about it."

"I would have said I was disappointed in you. I always had such high hopes."

"So did I, and I have no idea why. He never gave me any reason to hope. He was always honest with me. Emily's perfect for him. I like her."

Fayrene took five mugs from the cabinet and lined them up on the counter. "It was smart of you to go after Caleb, then."

"I didn't go after Caleb," Melanie protested. "He's just been helping me out. We're just friends."

"Mmm, hmm. If you say so, baby." she said with a big smile and wink.

"No, Mama," Melanie said firmly. "No, no, no. Caleb and I are friends. Best friends. Just like we've been all our lives."

"If you say so."

"What are you doing?" Melanie hissed.

Fayrene's purse had been sitting on the counter where she'd put it when she'd walked in the door that afternoon. She reached into it and pulled out a bottle of prescription medicine. She shook three capsules into her hand.

"It's time for someone to take a nap, don't you think?"

Melanie's eyes bulged. The dosage on the bottle said one capsule. "Is that for George? You'll kill him."

"Of course I won't." Then she frowned. "I don't think three will kill him. No, three won't kill him, I'm sure they won't. Besides, we have to counteract the caffeine, don't we?"

"Mama."

"Shh. Just remember, the Transylvania mug is his."

Melanie snapped her mouth shut. Their coffee mugs were all souvenirs from vacations, rodeos, cattle-buying trips, et cetera. When Melanie was in high school they'd gone through a little town in Louisiana named Transylvania. Everything in the town, she remembered, had a bat on it. The mug they'd brought home with them was no exception. A vampire bat.

"After all," Fayrene said, "it's as plain as Lucy and Ethel that he's nothing but a bloodsucker."

"Lucy and Ethel?"

Fayrene arched her back and stuck out her chest. "Baby, when they're this big they deserve names of their own."

"Mama, that's—" Melanie snickered. "That's awful."

"Whatever. He works for a bloodsucker, and he is a bloodsucker."

Melanie shook her head. Her mother had always had a sly, sneaky streak. "Shame on us. You pour, I'll serve."

It was all Caleb could do to keep from bouncing his knee in agitation. What were Melanie and her mother doing out there in the kitchen? How the hell long did it take to brew a pot of coffee, for crying out loud?

She was safer in the kitchen. If she stayed in the kitchen. But she was just crazy enough to try something foolish. What, Caleb couldn't imagine.

A moment later he let out a quiet breath when she walked into the living room carrying two mugs of coffee. She handed the first to him, then turned away before he could say thanks.

"George?" She crossed to the far end of the sofa where their keeper sat. "Do you want cream or sugar? We don't have cream, but we have milk and that fake powder stuff."

"Black's fine. Thanks. I really appreciate y'all taking this so well."

"No problem," she told him. "It's almost over, right?"

She was much too nice and accommodating, Caleb thought. She was up to something.

George blew on his coffee. "That's right. It's almost over."

Melanie turned away and went back to the kitchen. She returned a moment later with her own mug of coffee, and Fayrene followed with a mug for Ralph and herself.

Caleb nearly choked at the way Fayrene squirmed her rear in those skintight jeans as she sat down between her husband and the goon. He was almost positive that she brushed her breast against George's arm. The man nearly dropped his coffee.

"This is good," George said a moment later when he had steadied himself. "Everybody sitting around drinking coffee. This is good. I mean, it's not like anybody's being kidnapped or anything. I mean, Ralph here agreed to it, said it wouldn't be a problem. Isn't that right, Ralph?''

Ralph gave a grunt and took a sip of his coffee.

"Sure is good coffee, Mrs. Pruitt," George said.

"Thank you, George," she said with a little wiggle of her rear and shoulders.

"Kind of a nutty taste to it." He turned the mug up and drained it.

"It's a special blend I get in Phoenix," Fayrene told him.

Ralph looked down into his mug and frowned. "Tastes like plain ol' c-c-c—''

Fayrene twisted on the sofa until one breast rubbed against Ralph's arm. His words stuttered to a halt.

Caleb's head swam. Suspicious one minute, amused the next, he didn't know what to think or feel.

Then he was just plain stunned when George let out a small snore.

Fayrene smiled serenely and took the mug from his hand before it fell to the floor.

Ralph leaned forward to peer at George, on the other side of Fayrene. "What the hell? George?"

Fayrene patted Ralph's knee and pushed herself up from the sofa, George's mug in her hand. "He can't hear you, hon. He's sleeping like a baby."

"What have you done?" Ralph cried. "Good God, woman, what have you done?"

Fayrene gave a toss of her head. "I've fixed it so I can go to the bathroom in my own home without having to ask permission. That's what I've done."

Caleb nearly bobbled his mug.

Ralph gaped openmouthed as his wife left the room, headed for the bathroom.

"What did she do to him?" Ralph demanded of Melanie.

"She put sleeping pills in his coffee."

"Good God." He stared at the empty doorway another moment, then looked over at George, snoozing peacefully at the opposite end of the sofa. He shook his head. "Woman always was full of surprises."

"Okay." Fayrene had returned from the bathroom. She stood before the others in the living room and propped her hands on her hips. "Now what?"

"Are you out of your mind?" Ralph roared.

"Probably," she said tartly. "I'm here, aren't I?"

"How long will he be out?" Caleb asked, hoping to avoid a personal argument between husband and wife.

Fayrene shrugged. "I take one pill and I'm out for eight hours."

"How many did you give him?" Caleb asked.

She smiled. "Three. But don't forget the caffeine he drank. And he's bigger than I am."

"Any way you figure it," Melanie offered, "he's down for the count. Or at least until we wake him. Mama, I'm so proud of you I could pop my buttons." She threw her arms around her mother and kissed her.

"Proud of her? She might have killed this man," Ralph protested.

"Proud of her because now we can get out to that pickup and find out just what kind of merchandise has to be delivered and divvied up in the middle of the night."

"Are you going to argue about this?" Fayrene asked her husband.

"No," Ralph said slowly. "No, I'm not. I never bargained to have all of you held here against your will like this. I want you all to know I'm sorry about this. I have to go through with the deal to pay off my debt. But none of you should have to be involved. Truth is, I wouldn't have gone along with it at all if they hadn't threatened to put me in the hospital, and Melanie right along with me. But I don't see how we're going to do anything about it, unless you plan on drugging Little Donnie, too. And then what do we do when Bruno shows up? I owe him money. He takes money seriously.''

"Relax, Mr. Pruitt.'' Caleb placed a hand on Ralph's shoulder and squeezed. "The rest of you stay here in case Little Donnie comes up to the house for anything. I'll slip out a back window and go check out that pickup in the pasture.''

"Now wait just a minute,'' Melanie protested. "When I said *we* could go out there, I meant that figuratively, not literally. *I'm* going.''

"There's no need for you to go traipsing around outside in the middle of the night,'' Caleb claimed. "You'll stay here. I'm going.''

"Says who?''

"Says me.''

"You think just because you gave me the best orgasm of my life that I've suddenly become helpless? Or stupid? Or timid?''

"What?" Ralph bellowed. "Did you say…orgasm? As in *sex?"*

Fayrene fanned herself. "Oh, my.''

"Melanie,'' Caleb pleaded, keeping one eye on Ralph in case the man decided to grab George's gun and come after him.

"This time last week,'' Melanie declared hotly, "when all we were was best friends, you would never have questioned my going out there. You probably would have sent me on my own.''

"I would not.''

"You damn sure wouldn't have told me to stay in the house and keep safe, like some little idiot who can't take care of herself.''

"That's not what I meant,'' he protested.

"That's exactly what you meant. I used to be your friend. Now you see me as the little woman. Well, I won't have it, do you hear me? You don't tell me what to do, you don't protect me, you don't take care of my problems. You got that?''

He hated it when she was right. He was thinking of her differently. He couldn't help it. He'd held her, kissed her. Been inside her. How could he not want to see her safe and protected?

But that was his male ego talking. Melanie, he knew, would have none of it. If he wanted to keep her friendship and stay close to her, he was going to have to respect her in the ways she required in order for her to feel respected.

"I've got it,'' he told her. "You're right. I'm sorry. We'll go together.''

Melanie sneered. "Gee, thanks.''

"I don't suppose you could come up with a couple of flashlights, could you?'' He bowed from the waist and swept an arm out to his side. "That is, if you're through being sarcastic?''

"Oh, I've only just begun.''

"And a big screwdriver or something to pry open the back of the camper. I'm assuming they locked it.''

With a curl of her upper lip, Melanie marched to the pantry off the kitchen and came back a moment later with two flashlights and an eighteen-inch-long screw-driver.

"You'll need jackets," Fayrene said.

Ralph took a couple of jackets from the coat closet and handed them out.

They looked out the kitchen window and could see Little Donnie sitting in his car puffing on a cigarette, plumes of smoke gushing from the open driver's window.

"He's not going anywhere," Caleb muttered. "Let's go."

They left by way of the window in the den, which couldn't be seen from the front, back or driveway. They kept their flashlights turned off and let the glow of the utility light over by the barn light their way. Keeping the house between them and Little Donnie, they made their way past the garden and into the edge of the woods.

It was quiet enough that every footfall seemed to echo through the night, but there were still enough frogs in the trees and out around the ponds, even this late in the year, to create enough noise to cover the sounds of their passage.

Once in the woods they turned on their flashlights and followed the fence line over the rise and down into the pasture. Then they cut north toward the pickup parked beneath an oak on the far side.

They stopped and turned off their flashlights. There was enough moonlight to see where they were going.

"We're assuming there's no one there," Caleb said.

"Yeah."

"You know what assuming does."

"Yeah. It makes an *ass* out of *u* and *me*."

But there was no way to sneak up on the pickup.

There was nothing surrounding the tree under which it sat for a hundred yards in any direction except grass barely tall enough to hide a snake.

With no other choice, they walked openly across the pasture toward the truck filled with "goods."

Ten feet from the pickup Caleb grabbed Melanie's arm and put a hand over her mouth. Next to her ear he whispered, "Shh. Listen."

Melanie tried, but her heart was pounding too loudly. She strained to hear over the thunder in her ears.

Then she heard it. "Voices."

There were windows all around the camper shell, and of course the front and sides of the cab of the truck. Caleb and Melanie were approaching from the rear. Anyone in the camper would be able to see them.

But why would anyone be in the camper? That was where the goods, whatever they were, should be.

"Careful," Caleb whispered.

She nodded, and they crept closer.

"What's that smell?" she whispered. "Did something die?"

Caleb stopped and sniffed, then swore quietly. "I don't think so. Come on."

No shouts of alarm sounded as they neared the pickup. In fact, there was suddenly no sound at all, except, Melanie thought, the pounding of her heart.

They approached the back of the camper as quietly as possible. They checked the cab first and found it empty. They tried to see into the camper, using their flashlights, but the camper's windows had been covered with a reflective material. If they wanted to see inside, they were going to have to open it up.

Caleb reached for the handle of the door, and Melanie held her breath. He gave a yank, but the handle was locked. He paused and listened but heard nothing. That bothered him. He had definitely heard voices earlier.

Using the screwdriver, he pried the lock free at the sides of the camper door. Then, nodding to Melanie, he gripped the handle and flung open the door.

Melanie hit the button on her flashlight, but the smell struck them in the face before the beam illuminated the interior.

What they found shocked them both to the core.

Chapter Eight

People. The camper shell was crammed with people. And from the smell of things, they'd been in there entirely too long. Days too long. The stench was unbearable.

Melanie gasped and stepped back, covering her nose and mouth with her arm.

Caleb coughed.

From inside the camper, no one made a sound. They stared out at Melanie and Caleb like terrified statues. Four women, eight men, three children under the age of ten. Each adult clutched a cloth bundle. Four clear plastic gallon jugs that perhaps once held water but now held, well, other liquid. One five-gallon bucket and a half-dozen empty toilet-paper rolls. All crammed into the small camper space like the proverbial sardines in a can.

But it was the hope on the faces, even behind the

fear, that reached Melanie. A deep pity stirred inside her for the horrifying conditions.

Someone whispered, *"Una gringa."*

One man at the far end leaned forward. *"¿Los Estados Unidos?"*

"The U.S.?" another asked. "Are we in the United States?"

Melanie and Caleb shared a stunned look. "Yes," Melanie answered. "Oklahoma."

"Oklahoma? Truly? In America?"

"Yes," Melanie told the man. *"Sí.* In America. Where are you from?"

"Are you police?"

"No, no," Melanie said quickly. "No police. How…how long have you been here, in the pickup?"

"Two days," the man answered. "We come from Sonora, in Mexico. The man, he promise us jobs. Good jobs. We work for you?"

"Oh, uh, no, not for us."

"But we must work to pay for being brought here."

"What do you mean?"

"We each paid the man to bring us, but the cost was so high that none of us could pay it all. We work to pay the rest."

"Is it a lot of money?" Melanie asked.

"Sí. It is very much money. We paid five hundred U.S. dollars each, and now we work to pay the other two thousand."

"Dollars?" Melanie squeaked.

"Sí."

"Each?"

"Sí. We work for you now?"

"Not yet. It's too soon. You've only just arrived. Why don't you get out. If you want to."

"Is all right? That we get out?"

"Yes, yes. Please. Get out and be comfortable." Melanie grabbed Caleb's arm and dragged him aside. "Jobs? The Bruno McGuire Employment Agency? I don't think so. What's going on? What are we going to do? He'll find a way to use them and make their lives miserable."

"What is this?" Caleb hissed. "For somebody who doesn't like illegal aliens, you sound awfully concerned."

"Oh, stuff it. These people are in trouble."

"Maybe you're the one who's been running an underground railroad in the county."

"Maybe you've been sniffing locoweed. Bruno's going to turn these people into slaves."

"I'm afraid it's worse than that," Caleb whispered.

"What do you mean?"

"The kids."

"Yeah, I'm wondering about them, too. If he's bringing in illegal aliens to work, why would he bring families with small children?"

"Because he can take the children and hold them hostage, make the parents turn over all their pay. And he can sell the kids. Or rent them by the hour to perverts."

Melanie's stomach churned.

"They talk about this sort of exploitation all the time on the news."

"What are we going to do? We can't just let him take them away and turn them into virtual slaves."

"They're on your land. What do you want to do?"

"Oh, great. Now you decide to let me make the decisions."

"If you're asking what I'd do, I'd get them out of

here so Bruno can't find them. They're obviously illegals. It's not like he can complain to the cops, right?''

''No, he can just break Daddy's kneecaps.''

''There is that.''

''But not,'' Melanie said thoughtfully, ''if *we* complained to the cops.''

''You mean turn these people over to Immigration?''

Melanie swallowed. Of course, that was exactly what they should do. These poor people were in the U.S. illegally. Immigration would send them back to Mexico.

She looked at them, at their wretched condition, at the wretched conditions they'd suffered to find new jobs to feed their families. Yet they would work for Bruno for years and never pay off their debt, never even come close to the great American dream. Bruno's interest rates made credit card companies look like Santa Claus.

''No,'' Melanie said. ''Not unless we have no choice. But there is such a thing as home invasion, and my home has definitely been invaded. Before we do anything, we need to move these people. Hide them.''

''Where? Why?'' Caleb asked.

''We can hide them down at the hay barn,'' she said. ''As for why, because I'll be damned if Bruno is going to use the Pruitt Ranch in his disgusting scheme.''

Caleb smiled. ''That's my girl.''

''Huh. In your dreams, pal.''

''There, too. But we also have to think about your dad. We interfere in this, Bruno will take it out on him.''

''I know.'' She paced away, then back. ''I know. Daddy went along with this to cancel out his debt.''

"He went along with it to avoid getting his kneecaps broken. And maybe yours, too."

"I know, I know. But it's not like Daddy can get police protection from his bookie."

"No, but Bruno's not just going to go away. He lets your dad get away without paying and anybody hears about it, he loses his reputation, then his business."

"And I'd feel so sorry for him."

"Me, too. But nobody named Bruno is going to let that happen. He's going to come after your dad, or you're going to go out to the barn some morning and find another goon waiting out there."

Melanie threw her hands in the air. "What am I supposed to do about it?"

"The only thing you can do. The only thing he'll settle for. Pay him."

"I can't afford it," she cried.

"Melanie." He took her by the shoulders and held her still. "Are we friends?"

"Not for much longer if you don't get to the point."

"I can pay him."

"You cannot!"

"I can, and if you won't take it as a gift from one friend to another, you can pay me back later, whenever it's convenient."

"Caleb!"

"Melanie."

Melanie fought back a groan. "I can't deal with this right now. Let's just get these people out of here first. We'll worry about Daddy and the money later."

Melanie explained the situation as best she could, while those who spoke English translated for the others.

"The man, Bruno, who arranged to bring you here, is a bad man. He makes money off the misery of others. When he comes here in a little while he's going to separate you into two or three groups. It's possible he'll separate husbands from wives, and there will be nothing you can do about it. It's almost certain that he'll take the children away from their parents."

After the translations, one woman hugged her daughter close and spoke a rapid stream of Spanish that was far beyond Melanie's high-school-Spanish vocabulary.

"She asks," said the man who identified himself as Jorge, "why a man would do such a thing."

"Because he can, then force you to work even harder and give him every cent you earn. He'll tell you it's to take care of your children. He'll make you do things you won't want to do. If you don't do what he wants, he'll say you'll never see your children again. Meanwhile he'll be selling your children to other men, making them do things no child should ever have to do."

When Jorge translated, everyone spoke at once.

"Hitting them pretty hard, aren't you?" Caleb asked.

"I want them to understand the kind of man they're up against."

"You're scaring them."

"I mean to."

One woman started to wail.

"No." Melanie grabbed Jorge's arm. "Stop her. We have to keep quiet. Stop her now! They left a man, a lookout, just over the rise. We can't let him know you're out of the truck."

"Shh, shh," Jorge said, followed by a fast stream of Spanish.

The woman gasped and fell silent.

"Thank you," Melanie said. "The man on guard has a gun and I'd hate for him to come out here to investigate."

"A gun?"

"That's right. The other men who will come for you will have guns, too."

"What can we do? We came here to work, for our families. We want no trouble."

"We can hide you until the men leave."

Jorge looked around the empty pasture. "Hide us where?"

She pointed west. "There's a hay barn not far away. You'll be safe there."

"The owner, he will not mind?"

"This is my family's ranch. I'm one of the owners."

Caleb stepped up. "If Bruno decides to look around, he could easily find them there. They'll be safer on the Rose."

"Are you sure?" Melanie asked. "You don't mind?"

"What is this Rose?" Jorge asked.

"It's my ranch. The Cherokee Rose. You'll be safer there. It's not far, but if you're all willing, we should get moving."

They were willing. Eager, even, to avoid the men with the guns who would come for them.

Melanie led the way across the pasture and down along the fence. The Mexicans moved slowly; they were exhausted and hungry and had little strength left. The children staggered with fatigue. One woman was so weak she could barely walk and had to lean on her husband. Caleb brought up the rear.

How was a man supposed to keep up with a woman like Melanie? Figuratively speaking. Much less understand her. A couple of days ago she'd been all hot under the collar thinking he'd been breaking the law by helping illegal aliens.

Now look at her, he thought. Leading this group of ragtag refugees like Moses shepherding the Jews out of Egypt. Except Moses hadn't had a flashlight.

For this particular exodus, Caleb was grateful for the flashlights but wished they had a little more time. Or a little more speed. If Bruno and his men showed up and caught them out in the open, there was no telling what might happen.

The woman just ahead stumbled again. Her husband was getting weaker, having more trouble carrying her weight.

"Here," Caleb offered. "Let me take her for a while so you can catch your breath."

"Oh, *gracias, señor,* but I am able to manage." He straightened and adjusted his grip around his wife's back. The woman let out a soft moan.

Caleb fell back, but not too far, and followed, ready to leap forward and catch the woman if the man couldn't hold her up.

He figured they were another ten minutes away from their goal. Melanie hadn't said so, but he knew she was taking them to the gate she and Caleb had installed the other day. Trying to get these people through the barbed-wire fence, children included, without someone getting sliced up, would be nearly impossible. The gate would be much easier.

They finally reached the gate and made it through to the copse of blackjack trees on the Cherokee Rose on the other side. Caleb turned back to close the gate, and the woman who'd been having trouble let out a cry and sank to her knees.

"Maria!" Her husband fell to his knees beside her.

Caleb rushed over and dropped beside them. "What's wrong?"

"It's the baby, *señor*."

"Baby? What baby?"

"The one that is coming."

"Coming?" Caleb tried to swallow and couldn't. Surely he'd heard wrong. "What do you mean, coming?"

"What's all the noise about?" Melanie elbowed her way through the crowd surrounding the downed trio. "What's going on?"

Caleb looked up at her. The sky was gone, blocked out by tree branches still thick with leaves. Why in the name of all that was holy had he not brought a cell phone? His was in the front seat of his pickup and Little Donnie might have spotted him retrieving it, but Melanie's was in the pile of phones George had collected. Caleb's only excuse for such a lapse was that he didn't seem to think straight around Melanie these days. Didn't seem to be able to think much at all around her.

Now, here they were, out in the woods in the middle of the night with a baby on the way and no way to call for help.

"Unless I miss my guess," he answered Melanie, "we're having a baby."

"Oh my God." For a moment, Melanie's mind simply went blank. She dealt with birth on a regular basis on the ranch, of course, but not human birth. "How long has she been having pains?"

"I have no watch," the man with her said. "But it has been since a long time before we stopped."

"Are you her husband?" Melanie asked.

"*Sí.* I am Pedro Martinez. This is my wife Maria. This is our first baby."

"Maria, do you speak English?"

"She does not," Pedro said. "I am sorry."

Melanie looked over at Caleb. "How far are we from the house?"

"About a half mile."

She swore under her breath. "Too far to carry her."

Maria cried out and arched her body against a contraction. When it subsided she spoke to her husband in halting Spanish.

"She says the baby comes now."

"Oh, God. I don't suppose anyone here knows about childbirth." She looked up hopefully to the other three women.

Two women immediately shook their heads. They each took a child, one a young girl, the other a boy, by the hand and backed away. The third woman waited for Jorge to translate, then answered him.

"She says," Jorge told Melanie, "that all she knows how to do is push one out. She does not know about the catching, but how hard can it be? That is her question, not mine, *por favor.*"

"How hard can it be," Melanie muttered, trying to bite back her sarcasm. "Pushing and catching. Here's hoping it's that simple." Unless something went wrong, it should be that simple. Most births went smoothly, didn't they?

God, we could use a little help here.

"I can get to the house and have help back here within twenty minutes," Caleb said.

Melanie shot him a desperate glare. "If you think you can leave me here alone and not suffer the consequences, think again. Before anybody goes anywhere, somebody needs to see how far along she really is."

Caleb took a step back and raised both hands. "Don't look at me."

"Just like a man," Melanie muttered. "Okay, first let's make Maria comfortable. Caleb, give me your jacket." She took off her own and used both jackets to create a makeshift bed for Maria. A hell of a place to have a baby, on the ground in the dark beneath the trees in a foreign land. In forty-degree weather. Fleeing from the likes of Bruno McGuire and his goons.

If that weren't bad enough, it seemed the height of indignity to Melanie for a woman to have some stranger shine a flashlight up her skirt, but there seemed to be no help for it. Maria appeared to be in serious labor and Melanie had to see if the baby was crowning yet.

At least, she thought *crowning* was the word for what happened when the top of the baby's head started putting in an appearance.

And that was exactly what was happening underneath Maria's torn and filthy skirt when Melanie looked.

"I see the head," Melanie said, hoping her voice was steadier than her nerves.

Pedro squeezed his wife's hand and translated.

"Don't push."

"*¿Señora?*"

"*Señorita,*" Melanie corrected. "Tell Maria not to push. Not yet. Just pant through the pain. Don't worry,

Pedro, and tell Maria not to worry. Everything will be all right." From her lips to God's ears.

While Pedro repeated her words to his wife Melanie prayed she was right. She could see the next contraction contorting Maria's abdomen. "Breathe," she told the woman. "Little breaths. Pant." And she panted with her. And so did Pedro. And everyone else in the clearing.

When the pain ebbed and Maria began to relax, the panting stopped and everyone looked around and laughed sheepishly.

"She can't be moved," Melanie told Caleb. "It's too late."

Caleb knelt beside her, but turned at an angle that would not allow him to see beneath Maria's skirt. Melanie wondered whose modesty he was trying to preserve, Maria's, or his own.

"You seem to be okay with this," he said. "Where'd you learn about childbirth?"

"Never mind that." She didn't think anyone in the vicinity would appreciate hearing that everything she knew about childbirth she'd learned from the Discovery Health Channel.

"Looks like you don't need me. I should go to the house for help."

Melanie gripped his arm hard enough to cut off circulation in her fingers. "Don't you dare leave me," she hissed.

Maria groaned with another contraction.

"Pant," Melanie reminded her. "Little breaths. Don't push, don't push. The head's coming. Slowly, but it's coming. Just let it come. There it is." She held the baby's head gently in her hands and beamed, her heart pounding ninety to nothing.

Caleb's gaze was drawn to Melanie's hands against his will. He couldn't help but stare in awe at all that dark hair on such a tiny head.

Not, he thought, that Maria would consider it such a tiny head. Lord, what women had to go through to bring new life into the world.

When Maria's contraction eased, Melanie had Pedro sit behind his wife, propping her up to a semireclining position to help her push the child from her womb.

"This time," Melanie said, "when the next contraction comes, push as hard as you can. And don't worry about being quiet. You tell her that, Pedro. Tell her she can scream as loud as she wants."

One of the other women spoke to Maria, and Maria answered, gesturing toward the cloth bundle she'd been carrying. The other woman opened the bundle and pulled out a small blanket.

"For the baby," Pedro said.

Melanie smiled at him, and at Maria. "It's lovely. You'll be needing it in just a few minutes." She handed her flashlight to the other woman and had her aim the beam between Maria's thighs.

Caleb felt the tension emanating from Melanie, but bless her, she didn't let it show. Both her voice and manner were easy and calm. His admiration for this woman he'd known all his life rose to new heights.

How many new things, he wondered, could a man learn about a woman he thought he knew?

"Caleb?" Melanie said. "I need a hand here."

A hand? She had to be kidding. He followed her line of sight and felt his throat close. The umbilical cord was wrapped around the baby's neck.

"I'll hold his head up," she said. "You slip the cord over it."

Caleb took a deep breath and felt a sense of calm settle over him that he had not felt in hours. Melanie needed him. This baby and its mother needed him. With a steady hand he slipped a finger beneath the cord and eased it up over the head. "There you go," he said.

"Thanks. Okay, here we go, Maria. Push hard."

Caleb stared in awe as Melanie held the baby's head and a shoulder popped free. A moment later, accompanied by a strangled cry from Maria, the other shoulder emerged.

"I could use another hand here," Melanie said.

Caleb leaned closer and put his hand beneath the baby's shoulder while Melanie held the head. After that, the baby just seemed to slip right out into their waiting hands as if there had been no effort involved at all by anyone. It was the most miraculous sight Caleb had ever witnessed. He felt awed. Humbled. Exuberant.

"It's a girl," Melanie whispered, her voice filled with the same reverence that Caleb felt.

"Here." Caleb gently ran a thumb and forefinger down the tiny nose to help clear out the mucus. He rolled the baby over in Melanie's hands and tapped on her little back. The baby let out a small mewl of protest, then a loud, boisterous cry.

The small clearing in the woods erupted with laughter and cheers.

Caleb looked into Melanie's eyes and felt a connection as deep as the one they'd shared when they'd made love.

Then the baby squirmed and broke the moment.

With a nervous laugh Melanie placed the baby on Maria's belly and barely remembered the afterbirth in time to catch it when it came out a moment later. She tucked it up next to the baby and wrapped them both in the blanket Maria had brought for her newborn.

"Here she is, Maria, Pedro. Your daughter. Do you realize she's a U.S. citizen?"

Pedro gasped. "Truly?"

"Truly. Born in the U.S.A. Right here on the Cherokee Rose ranch in the middle of Oklahoma, the center of the whole country."

Quiet tears streamed down the new father's face as he repeated this news in Spanish for his wife.

Maria held her daughter against her, with Pedro's arms around them both, and cried tears of joy and exhaustion.

"You do good work," Caleb told Melanie.

She squeezed his hand. "*We* do good work. I guess you can go for help now. We'll need to cut the cord, but I'd feel better if Rose and Emily were here before we tried to move her. She needs padding and blankets and water and—"

"I get the idea. I'll hurry." Before he stood up, he leaned over and kissed her hard on the mouth. "You're really something, you know that?"

She grinned. "So are you, pal. Now, get going. See how fast those boots can carry you."

His boots carried him as fast as they could, but, damn, they were not made for running, particularly on rough ground. They were made for holding a man's footing in the stirrups. They were made for dancing a two-step or the Cotton-Eyed Joe. They were made for kicking butt. And okay, they were made for looking cool. They were not made for running.

By the time he broke through the trees and saw the

yard light ahead in the distance, he was starting to breathe hard. He had to crawl through one barbed-wire fence, then cut across the corner of a pasture. A final fence, then the gravel driveway to the house.

He let himself in the back door.

The house had four bedrooms upstairs and what they used to call the guest room downstairs behind the kitchen. Since Sloan and Emily married, Justin had moved downstairs to the guest room so Emily's daughters, Janie and Libby, could have the room next to their parents upstairs. Caleb had the third room, and their grandmother the fourth.

Caleb went to Justin's room first and woke him up, thankful to find him home and not out somewhere on an all-nighter.

"Wake up, kid, we've got a problem. Get dressed while I get Sloan and Grandmother."

Justin groaned. "You're gonna wake Grandmother in the middle of the night? Either it's damn serious or you've lost your mind."

"Probably a little bit of both."

When he ran upstairs he made sure to make plenty of noise, clomping extra hard on the risers. He didn't like surprising people in their bedrooms in the middle of the night. He preferred they hear him coming.

When everyone but Janie and Libby was downstairs in the kitchen, Caleb finally explained.

"I need your help. Melanie and I do. But before you agree, you have to know you'll be breaking the law."

Justin perked up instantly. "Do tell."

"Is it a big law, this one we'll be breaking?" Grandmother asked, straight-faced.

That pretty much broke the ice, as well as announced

the family's decision to help. Caleb had never been more grateful for and proud of his family.

He told them as quickly and briefly as possible about the Mexicans, the baby and the need for speed.

Rose stood and instantly began issuing orders for items to take with them to retrieve the Mexicans, and in particular the new mother and baby, and bring them to the house. She determined that Emily would be more useful helping her and Melanie with mother and child, but since someone had to stay home in case the girls woke, Justin was assigned that job.

He didn't get a chance to protest being left out of the excitement before Rose gave him a list of instructions as long as his arm: gather all the blankets, extra clothes and anything else their guests might need. Start making sandwiches and don't stop until he had three dozen.

There was more, but Caleb left it to Justin to worry about. He went out and started up the SUV they would use to bring Maria and her baby to the house. Sloan would drive the pickup to carry the others.

The baby would be called Rosa, after the American ranch where she'd been born.

When Caleb heard that upon his return to the woods, he smiled curiously at Melanie. "Did you think that one up?"

"Not on your life. It was Maria and Pedro. Caleb, you wouldn't believe how excited they are that their daughter is an American citizen."

Caleb took her hand and pulled her aside. "Won't she have to have a birth certificate for that to be official?"

"I don't know," Melanie said. "But we'll figure it out."

He smiled. "We? You're really getting into this, aren't you?"

"Yeah, like you're not? Like it doesn't make you feel good to help these people?"

"I confess. Yes, it makes me feel good," Caleb said. "But we better leave everything else tonight to my family, so you and I can get back to your family before Bruno shows up and finds his 'goods' have disappeared."

"You know, if I thought about it too much," Melanie said, "it could really scare me how often you and I think alike."

Melanie introduced Maria to Rose and Emily and helped them clean her up and get her and the baby ready to move. Caleb then carried Maria through the woods to the SUV where he placed her, with the baby in her arms, on the blankets waiting for them in the back. Pedro climbed in beside her.

Melanie helped Sloan herd the others into the bed of the pickup he'd brought.

"What will happen to us now?" Jorge asked her.

"I don't know," she told him honestly. "But I don't want you to worry. We'll figure something out." While Caleb had been gone, Jorge had told her that some of them had family in New Mexico, others in Texas. "Maybe we can find your families here in the States. Or help you find jobs."

"Oh, that would be very good."

Melanie hoped so, but she worried about how they would be able to avoid the long arm of Immigration. The one saving grace for the Mexicans was that Immigration had most of their attention focused these days on other nationalities.

When both vehicles were loaded and everyone was ready to go, Sloan stopped Caleb and Melanie.

"Are you going to need some help when this Bruno character shows up and finds these people missing?" he asked.

"We wouldn't turn it down if you're offering."

"You don't want to call the sheriff?"

"No," Melanie said quickly. "No sheriff if we can help it. I'd rather nobody got a hint of these people."

"All right," Sloan said with a nod. "What do you want us to do?"

They discussed ideas and settled on the simplest. At a prearranged signal to Sloan's cell phone, Sloan and Justin would rush in.

"Just the two of them?" Melanie said when she and Caleb made it back to the PR side of the fence beyond the trees. "Is this going to work?"

"I guess that'll depend on how many men Bruno brings with him," Caleb said.

"Which we won't know until they show up and storm the house, demanding to know where their aliens went."

"Don't worry." He reached out and took her hand. "We won't be helpless. There are four of us even without Sloan and Justin."

"Don't worry," she mimicked. "How can I not worry? Are we doing the right thing?"

"It's a little late to ask that, isn't it?" He squeezed her hand gently.

His hand surrounding hers, holding it, steadied her. "Yes, definitely too late. And useless. We are doing the right thing. The only thing we can do. When you showed up this afternoon I was mad at you for not staying home."

"Were you?"

"I didn't want you to get caught up in our problems. I wouldn't have asked for your help."

"Melanie." He stopped in the moonlight and turned her to face him. "If I had a problem and you thought you could help, would you wait to be asked to help?"

"That's—"

"Of course you wouldn't. You saw a problem Saturday night at the party, and it was headed right at me." He grinned. "You didn't wait for me to ask for help, you just jumped to my rescue."

"Yeah, and look where it got us."

"I am." He slid his arms around her waist and pulled her close. "It got us out here alone in the moonlight." He dipped his head lower. "Just the two of us, right near the place where we made love this morning."

"Stop it." Melanie turned her head away and stepped out of his embrace. "All this sex business between us is just going to screw up our friendship. You're my best friend, the only one I can really talk to. You're the only person who believes in me and takes my side, no matter what. I don't want to lose that for sex, no matter how great the sex."

"Sex?" He took a step closer. "You think this is just about sex? Maybe for you, but for me it's more than that."

"I just think we need to take a big step back." And she did just that, and hated herself for it. "Look how you tried to protect me earlier by telling me to stay at the house. You're already treating me differently after just one time together."

"I can't help it if I want to keep you safe," he claimed.

"You're not in charge of my safety," she proclaimed heatedly. "That's what I'm talking about."

Caleb felt her slipping away from him. It wasn't only her words. Words could be argued with. But how did a man argue with hunched shoulders and eyes that wouldn't meet his? "Dammit, Melanie, look at me."

When she didn't, he felt a sense of desperation that threatened to swamp him. He grasped her arms and said it again. "Look at me. This is me, Melanie. The one who's been right beside you all this time. How many more years do I have to wait while you bounce from one man to another looking for something that's been right in front of you your whole life?"

"What?" she demanded, clearly shocked. "Wait. Back up. How many *more* years? Who are you trying to kid? You haven't been waiting on me for anything."

"Haven't I? I didn't realize it myself until just recently." Not until that day, in fact. Perhaps that very moment. "Yes, I've been waiting for you to look at me, to notice me. To love me."

Chapter Nine

A shiver of sheer terror raced down Melanie's spine. Love him? He was waiting for her to love him?

What was she supposed to do? How was she supposed to know what she was feeling? How was she supposed to know what love was and if it was real?

All those years she'd thought she loved Sloan, but whatever it was she'd been feeling—adoration, hero worship, puppy love—had not been the love a woman should feel for a man. She hadn't been concerned so much that *he* be happy. Instead she had believed that having him for her very own would make *her* happy. That was not the basis for a lasting love.

Thinking about all of this, particularly now, in the midst of their present circumstances with the Mexicans and Bruno and her parents, was giving her a pounding headache.

She pressed her hands to her temples. "Why can't we just be friends?"

Caleb knew she was afraid. Hell, so was he. But he also knew she felt more than friendship for him or she never would have given herself to him the way she did in the sunshine that morning.

Oh, she might have sex with a man now and then. A woman had needs, just as a man did. Then, too, she'd had to prove to herself and to whoever else she felt needed proof last year that she was, indeed, over Sloan. She'd spent the night with some joker from the next county, and then had never seen the man again. Caleb would be damned if she would dismiss him the same way.

But that wasn't sex he and Melanie had shared that morning. No, they hadn't had sex, they had made love, and she had cried in his arms because she'd been overwhelmed by emotion.

"Why can't we be just friends?" he asked. "Because of this." And he kissed her. Not a peck on the cheek or a friendly brush of lips, but an all-out lip-locking, breath-stealing, mind-numbing kiss.

Melanie's head reeled. It had been so long since she'd tasted him. Hours and hours since they'd shared a real kiss. She hadn't known how much she had craved it.

It was weak of her, wasn't it, to want a man this badly? Was she doomed to fool herself, to *make* a fool of herself for another ten or fifteen years over yet another Chisholm?

But she wasn't a child this time. There was no one urging her to please him, to eat her vegetables, tie ribbons in her hair, rope that steer faster so Caleb will like her better.

This time there was only Caleb and her. Just the two of them, and she didn't think she had the nerve to open herself to him the way he seemed to want. What if she opened herself, and there was nothing there?

She was afraid to find out.

He wanted too much from her. She wasn't brave enough to love him. She got along just fine without being in love, didn't she? Why did things have to change?

She pulled away from him and stepped back. Her chest was heaving, trying to supply air to her lungs.

"I'm going home," she said. "We've been gone too long."

He let her go, reluctantly, it seemed. She turned away, and in that last glimpse of him in the moonlight she saw in his eyes that she had hurt him.

She stopped, hung her head.

He walked past her and kept going.

"Caleb, wait. I'm sorry."

"Me, too." But he kept walking.

A new fear seized Melanie. What if she was wrong? What if these confused and confusing feelings she had for Caleb meant she was truly in love with him? What if this was her last chance with him? What if she hurt him, pushed him away one too many times and he let her put distance between them, let her hold him at arm's length?

Was that what she wanted? To lean on him but never hold him again? To confide in him rather than kiss him? To shake his hand or slap him on the shoulder as one good friend might do to another, instead of making sweet hot love the way they'd done that morning?

Or, maybe, if she pushed him away hard enough and far enough, to lose him altogether.

Oh, God, no. She couldn't imagine her life without him. Didn't that mean something?

"Caleb, I'm sorry. Wait. Please?"

Ten paces ahead, he slowed to a stop.

Melanie rushed to his side. "Please don't be angry with me," she begged.

He let out a long breath. "I'm not angry."

"I'm scared, Caleb. You want something from me I'm not sure I can give you."

He turned and cupped his hands on her shoulders. "All I want is for you to be yourself, Melanie. Just be honest with me, and with yourself. That's all."

"No." She smiled sadly. "That's not all, but even if it were, it's not so easy a thing you ask, for me to be honest with myself. That's the part that scares me. Can we just…"

"Be friends?"

"I was going to say take it slow, so I don't feel quite so much like I'm in over my head with you. I don't want to hurt either one of us, and I'm afraid I will."

He let out another long breath and slipped one arm around her shoulder and started them walking again toward her house. "Sure, we can take it slow. But, Melanie, the one thing I don't want you to do is hurt yourself. I don't ever want that."

As they topped the rise and the house appeared two hundred yards ahead, the true meaning of his words sank in. He loved her that much, that he would rather she hurt him than herself. No man had ever loved her that much before. It made her feel all soft and quivery inside. Her eyes stung and her heart hurt.

What did a woman do when she was loved by a man like Caleb Chisholm?

That question echoed over and over inside her head

as they crept quietly along the fence and came up to the house at the angle that would keep them hidden from Little Donnie.

She was still pondering the question as Caleb pushed open the window in the den and gave her a leg up. She crawled through into the room as quietly as possible, hearing nothing but the television from the living room.

It was as she straightened and turned back toward the window that the truth hit her, and when it came, it seemed so simple, so inevitable and natural, that it took her breath away.

Suddenly she leaned out the window. "Caleb?"

"What's wrong?"

"Nothing," she whispered, shaking her head. "I just wanted to tell you I love you, too."

While he stood there and gaped, she ducked back inside the room and rushed out to find her parents before she had to face Caleb again. She'd said the words and meant them. But what if she'd been wrong and they weren't what he'd wanted from her? What if he was standing out there right now laughing because she thought he loved her? He hadn't actually said he loved her. He'd said he wanted her to love him. There was a big difference. Wasn't there?

A woman could go crazy thinking about such things.

Okay, so she loved him. That didn't have to change everything, did it? They could still be friends. They'd just be closer friends than before. Intimate friends.

That had a nice ring to it. Intimate friends. A little on the hollow side, but a nice ring, nonetheless.

Caleb stood outside the open window, too stunned for a moment to do more than stare at the empty spot that had, only an instant before, held Melanie's face.

Had she really said she loved him, or had it all been in his head, because he'd had a sharp, burning need to hear those words from her.

There was only one way to find out. He practically dived through the window, only to find the den empty. He found her in the living room explaining to her parents what had been happening.

George was still slumped in the corner of the sofa, snoring lightly.

"And she had the baby right there on the ground," Melanie said.

"In the woods?" Fayrene gasped. "That poor woman."

"I'll say. With nobody to help her but Caleb and me. Oh, Caleb, there you are. I was just—"

"What did you just say?" he asked carefully.

Melanie pursed her lips. "There you are?"

He narrowed his eyes. "Before that."

"Maria had the baby on the ground in the woods?"

"Melanie."

"Later."

"Is there something the two of you would like to share with us?" Fayrene asked.

"No," they said in unison.

Ralph shook his head. "Illegal aliens, right here on the PR. What was Bruno thinking?"

"That he was going to get away with it," Caleb said.

"I'm sorry, Daddy, but we couldn't leave those people there. That leaves you in a bad spot with Bruno."

"Well, I'm not going to just lie down for him, now, am I?" He reached behind the sofa and hefted a shotgun. "I owe him the money, and I should pay him. But I should never have agreed to this. I won't have my family threatened and held hostage. I won't have my ranch used this way. I thought it would be stereos or computers or something, and that would have been bad enough. But people, no way.''

"You were coerced," Melanie said.

"Threatened," Caleb added. "Got another shotgun?"

"Oh, Lord." Fayrene started fanning herself. "I think I might faint."

"Faint, my aunt Fanny." Ralph chuckled at her. "You're the one who drugged the fellow with the gun."

"Why, Ralphie." Fayrene patted his arm. "You say that like you're almost proud of me."

"Of course I'm proud of you, darlin'." He patted the hand she'd left on his arm and kissed her cheek. Then he passed a pistol to her and another to Melanie. "Now, we better be figuring out what we're gonna do."

After several minutes of discussion, during which they more or less decided they didn't know what they were going to do, Ralph proclaimed that he was in charge. It was his house, his ranch and his debt. Therefore, his problem.

"While Sleeping Beauty here is still snoring away, I want the rest of you to sneak out the back, like the two of you did earlier, and stay away from the house until Bruno and his crew have come and gone."

"And leave you here alone?" Fayrene cried.

"Shh," he warned. "You'll wake up George."

"We're not leaving you," Melanie stated firmly.

"We can signal for help whenever we need it," Caleb told him. "If you can talk the ladies into leaving, power to you, but I'm staying. You can't take on

George, Little Donnie, Bruno and whoever else he brings with him.''

Melanie narrowed her eyes. "Did I hear you just suggest—''

"That we all stay,'' Caleb said in a rush.

Melanie beamed. "Smart man.''

"I'm learning.''

Ralph glanced across the room toward the kitchen. "Looks like talking time's up. Here comes somebody.''

They rushed to the kitchen in time to see two pickups, each with a camper shell, drive past the barn and head toward the pasture.

"Well,'' Caleb said. "Shouldn't be long now.'' If he said he wasn't worried, he'd be lying. He pulled out his grandmother's cell phone and called Sloan with the prearranged signal. It was time to line up the reinforcements.

Sloan and Justin had said they would head to the PR, by way of the back woods, as soon as they got their new guests back to the house. The signal was to let them know to hurry, in case they hadn't left home yet. The plan was for them to slip into the house by way of the same window Caleb and Melanie had used, the window Caleb had left open.

Caleb's brothers would come armed, but they knew to come quietly, stealthily, and not barge in without knowing what was going on. The last thing anyone wanted was for someone to get hurt, and with the number of guns already in the house, not to mention those that soon would be, someone getting hurt was an all too likely possibility.

Still, Ralph was right to have the guns ready. When a rattlesnake slithered into your house you didn't wait to see what his intentions were before protecting yourself.

Having already taken George's gun away from him, Ralph now walked over and kicked the man's foot. "Wake up, George. Wake up. Bruno's here."

George blinked his eyes open and looked around, clearly confused. Slowly he pushed away from the back of the sofa until he was sitting upright on the edge. "What happened?" He scrubbed his face with both hands.

Ralph stood facing him on the opposite side of the coffee table. "You fell asleep."

George stared up at him blankly. "I what?"

"Here." Fayrene brought in a fresh mug. "Have some coffee. It'll wake you up."

When everybody chuckled, George frowned. He took the mug from Fayrene and stared at it. "Did I…? Never mind." He took a sip, then nearly dropped the mug when he spotted the shotgun dangling from Ralph's hand. "What the hell?" He looked this way and that, from his lap to the sofa to the floor, moving and jerking so fast he sloshed coffee over the back of his hand and yelped.

"If you spill any more of that I'll make you sorry," Fayrene warned. "I'll not have my sofa and carpet ruined by the likes of you."

"I'd pay attention to her if I were you." Ralph smiled at George. "I learned a long time ago never to upset her when she's armed."

From his spot in the wide doorway between the living room and kitchen, Caleb shook his head and chuckled silently. The things a man learned about his neighbors when he popped in on them uninvited.

A few hours ago Ralph had looked like a whipped

puppy. Now he was his old self again, steady and sure and not in the mood to take any crap from anyone. That was the Ralph Pruitt Caleb had known all his life. The man who'd raised Melanie into the intriguing, infuriating, marvelous woman she'd become.

The woman in question, with pistol in hand, strolled over to his side. "What's that look mean?"

He smiled. "What look would that be?"

"Oh, I don't know. Like maybe you just won the lottery."

"Didn't I?"

She smiled, then glanced out the window over the sink. Her smile faded. "We'll discuss it later, if we're still in one piece. Here they come. There's three pickups now. They brought the one that was already out there."

"Ralph," Caleb called. "It's time. Where do you want us?"

"George, you come with me. Have a seat there at the kitchen table. And keep your mouth shut."

"Man, are you crazy?" George jumped up and rounded the coffee table to confront Ralph. "What do you think you're doing? You're almost home free with Bruno. Why do you want to go and mess it up?"

"You don't need to worry about it." Ralph raised the shotgun one-handed and motioned toward the kitchen. "Just get in there and sit down."

"Bruno's not gonna like this, Pruitt."

"You think?"

"They're driving out to talk to Little Donnie," Caleb said, looking out the kitchen window. "I don't suppose we could be so lucky as to have them all just drive away. Nope. Here they come." When the three campers parked next to Caleb's pickup, doors popped open, men piled out. "I count three," Caleb said. "One's staying in the pickup. Little Donnie stayed at the driveway. We'll need to keep an eye on them so they don't surprise us."

"You people are toast," George said with a growl. "All of you."

No one bothered to answer him.

The back door burst open and in came three men. The one in the lead was the biggest, both in height and girth and hair. He stood about six foot two and weighed at least two-fifty. His carrot-orange hair stuck out around his head like a giant red afro. When he walked he rolled from side to side like a man striding the deck of a wave-tossed ship.

This, Caleb knew, had to be Bruno McGuire. He looked every bit as Irish as his last name indicated. To go with his orange-red hair he had blue eyes, fair skin and more freckles than an Appaloosa had spots. And he was definitely the man in charge. Or rather, thought he was.

"What the hell's going on around here?" he demanded, gaping at the guns pointing at him.

Melanie stood in the doorway to the living room with her pistol. Ralph stood next to the kitchen table, shotgun aimed at Bruno. Caleb leaned against the sink. He covered the two men behind Bruno. Fayrene was their backup, standing hidden in the dark pantry behind the men who had just barged in, a big honking Colt .45 held steady in her hands.

"You look surprised, Bruno." Ralph stared at his bookie dead on.

"There's no need for guns, Pruitt."

"Are you going to tell me you and your men aren't armed? You all just keep your hands in plain sight."

"I don't want any trouble here," Bruno said. "You and me had a deal, Pruitt. Are you welching?"

"I never welch on a bet," Ralph protested. "I owe you money, and I'll pay it. I don't know how, but I will. You had no call to threaten me and my family into going along with this business tonight."

"It was just a simple merchandise drop," Bruno complained.

"Your man here," Ralph said, nodding toward George, "held a gun on my little girl."

"And his little girl," Melanie said, sauntering forward, "didn't like it. She also didn't like what she found in the back of your pickup. She especially didn't like your using this ranch to smuggle what amounts to slaves. I mean, stereos or computers or cigarettes I could have tolerated. But not people. Poor people desperate enough to believe the lies they were told about what waited for them here."

Everything would have been all right, Caleb thought, if Melanie had stopped where she stood. Instead, she took one more step, putting her within reach of George, still seated where Ralph had ordered him, at the kitchen table.

Even as Caleb opened his mouth to warn her, it was too late. She put herself within inches of George.

George gave her a hard shove directly toward Bruno. Melanie's gun went flying, hit the refrigerator and landed on the floor. Melanie landed against Bruno.

Not one to miss an opportunity, Bruno spun her around and twisted her arm up behind her back.

Melanie cried out in surprise and pain.

"Drop your guns," Bruno ordered. "Or I'll break her arm. Do it!"

"Just take it easy," Caleb said. "There's no need to get excited."

"Excited? I've got two guns pointed at me."

"Now you know how we felt today," Ralph said.

"Put 'em down!" Bruno jerked Melanie's arm again.

"All right." Caleb couldn't stand seeing her face contort in pain. "Ralph?"

"Yeah. Okay, we're putting 'em down. Turn her loose."

"Put 'em down first."

Caleb and Ralph placed their shotguns on the floor. Caleb had no idea what Fayrene was doing, as the pantry was too dark.

The instant their guns were down, the two men with Bruno pulled pistols from beneath their jackets and covered the room.

"Okay," Caleb said. "You've got control. Now let her go."

"First, tell me where my merchandise is."

"What?" George jumped up from his chair. "They're—I mean it's—gone? Are you sure?"

"What do you take me for, an idiot? The camper's empty. The lock's broken. From the outside," Bruno added, glaring at Ralph. "What did you do?"

"What I did," Ralph said, "was change my mind. Our deal's off."

"Off?" Bruno bellowed. "Off? Nobody backs out of a deal with Bruno McGuire and walks away."

"I'll just have to find some other way to pay you," Ralph told him.

"You said you didn't have any money."

"I don't," Ralph admitted. "But I'll find some somewhere."

"Where's my merchandise?"

"It's gone," Ralph said calmly.

"Gone?" The freckles on Bruno's face stood out in sharp relief. "What do you mean gone? Gone where?"

"That's not important."

"The hell it's not. You better tell me." Bruno tightened his hold on Melanie. "And I mean right this damn minute, Pruitt. I'm through being nice to you. I want my merchandise, and I want my money."

"You're not getting them," Caleb said.

"Who the hell are you? This is between me and Pruitt."

Caleb clenched his fists at his sides. "Let her go."

"Let her go," Ralph said, "or you get nothing."

"Take her, then." Bruno shoved her away, hard.

She stumbled.

Caleb sprang forward and caught her. "Are you all right?"

Panting slightly, she nodded. "Just dandy."

"Now, where's my merchandise?"

Melanie had heard all she could stand from this bully. She turned around in Caleb's arms and faced Bruno. "They aren't *merchandise,* you bloodsucker, they're *people.*"

"They're *mine.* I want them back."

"They're gone," she told him. "It's not like you're even out any money, considering what they paid for the ride."

"Gone where? I want them back."

Melanie stepped from Caleb's embrace. He started to hold her back but didn't want to start a struggle just then. But when she took another step toward Bruno, he had to fight himself to keep from leaping after her.

"You can't have them," Melanie hissed.

"If you don't tell me exactly where they are, somebody here is going to get hurt." For the first time, Bruno himself pulled a pistol from beneath his jacket. He aimed the gun at Melanie's head. "You wanna be first?"

"Maybe *you* want to be first." Fayrene appeared out of the darkness behind Bruno's back, pressed the barrel of her .45 to the back of Bruno's neck, and cocked the gun. "I don't like men who threaten my baby. Gentlemen, your guns on the floor, please, or your boss is going have a real pain in the neck."

Bruno sneered at Ralph. "You let your women do your speaking and your fighting for you?"

Ralph grinned. "Every chance I get."

"That's usually enough," came Sloan's voice from the living-room doorway, "but every now and then his neighbors like to get in on the game. Guns on the floor, gentlemen."

Caleb's knees nearly buckled in relief. Leave it to Sloan to have such perfect timing. Justin was with him, of course, but when their grandmother stepped up between them with her Winchester .30–.30 deer rifle, Caleb hooted.

Seeing the new firepower aimed their way, Bruno and his men dropped their weapons to the floor.

"And don't expect any help from those two yahoos outside," Justin offered with a cheesy grin. "They're going to be tied up for a while."

"Welcome, neighbors," Ralph said. "'Preciate the visit."

"You would do the same for us," Rose said easily.

"Anytime," Ralph said. "Anyplace."

Before anything else happened, Caleb and Melanie gathered up all the discarded weapons: two shotguns and four pistols. Of the original two groups involved, Fayrene was the only one who managed not to be disarmed.

"Now see what you've done," Bruno said to Ralph. "All you had to do was pay your debt in the first place and none of this would have happened."

Ralph nodded. "You're right, of course."

"Who cares if he's right?" Melanie said fiercely. "Just because you owed him money doesn't give him the right to send his creeps snooping around in our barn when they think no one's around."

"When did this happen?" Ralph demanded.

"Never mind that," Melanie said.

"Twice in the past few weeks," Caleb supplied. "When she was here alone."

Ralph flushed in anger. "I'm sorry, Mel. I wish you'd told me."

"Forget that for now. Your debt didn't give him the right to do that, and it didn't give him the right to threaten you into letting him use this place to smuggle illegal aliens into the country."

Bruno started blustering, but Melanie cut him off.

"Here's how it's going to be, Bruno. You're going to get the money Daddy owes you, and you're going to leave this ranch and never come back. You're going to write off the Mexicans as a loss, even though you didn't lose a dime, you actually made money off them. You're not going to look for them, and if you accidentally find them you're not going to threaten them or harm them in any way. Do you have a problem with any of that?"

"You're damn right I do. I paid to have that merchandise brought in. It's mine and I want it."

Melanie remembered the hideous condition she and

Caleb had found those poor people in. She walked to the counter where they'd placed all the weapons and picked up her revolver. She aimed it at Bruno's head and said, "If you say one more word about those people, just one more, I'm going to shoot you between your shifty little eyes. Same goes if you or anyone you know comes near this ranch or my family or those people again."

A trickle of sweat made its way down Bruno's left temple, but he managed a credible sneer, looking as if his dearest dream was to get his hands around her throat. "You're bluffing."

With her right thumb, Melanie cocked the hammer on her revolver. "Am I?"

There was a taut moment of silence but for the hum of the refrigerator. Then Fayrene stepped forward and patted Melanie's shoulder. "Heaven knows the cockroach deserves killing, baby, but think of the mess we'd have to clean up. You know how you hate to clean the kitchen."

Always helpful, Justin piped up. "If you're really set on shooting him, Mel, we can take him outside. That way you wouldn't have to clean up anything."

"And if you shoot him," Sloan added, "you won't have to worry about him anymore."

Ralph chuckled. "As much as I appreciate all the suggestions, I guess we should stop teasing these fellows and send them on their way. The sooner I've seen the last of them the better I'll like it."

Bruno snarled. "You won't see the last of me until I get my money and my—"

"Ah-ah-ah," Melanie said. "You weren't going to mention something that as far as you're concerned no longer exists, were you? No, of course you weren't. You didn't get where you are today by being stupid.''

"Where he is right now?'' Fayrene asked. "You mean, in the kitchen, being held at gunpoint by a couple of women?''

"All right, girls,'' Ralph said. "That's enough. Let's let these gentlemen be on their way.''

Melanie heaved a sigh of disappointment. "Okay, Daddy, if you're not going to let me shoot him.''

"That's a good girl,'' Ralph told her.

"But before they leave, wait just a minute.'' Melanie dashed out of the room. She was back a moment later and handed Bruno a check.

"What's this?'' Bruno asked, incredulous.

"It's what Daddy owes you. You're all paid up now, so we won't be seeing you again. Right?''

"A check?'' he cried. "You expect me to take a check?''

"It's good. It won't bounce.''

Bruno laughed. "Honey, I'm a bookie. Bookies deal strictly in cash.''

"Well, this time you'll take a check.''

"Cut your losses,'' Caleb told him. "This is the best offer you'll get around here.''

The family didn't wait for Bruno to agree. They ushered him and his men out the door and kept their guns at the ready until all the bad guys had driven away.

When Bruno and his men were gone, Fayrene offered to fix breakfast for everyone, but Sloan, Justin and Rose thanked her and declined. They needed to get back to help Emily with the Mexicans.

Ralph offered his hand to Justin, Sloan, then Rose.

"I can't thank you enough for what you did for me tonight."

Rose waved his thanks away. "Don't think a thing of it, Ralph. That's what friends and neighbors are for."

"Still…" Ralph hung his head and blushed.

"Don't go getting all embarrassed, Ralph," she told him. "Not with me. A little gambling debt's nothing to worry about. My grandfather was hanged for a horse thief."

"I never knew that," Melanie said.

"It's true," Rose declared. Then she turned to Caleb. "Are you coming home with us?"

"Not just now," he told her.

"That's fine, then." She put her hand on Caleb's shoulder and added softly, "She'll make the perfect addition to the family." She winked and walked away with his brothers.

"What did she say?" Melanie asked.

Caleb smiled. "Nothing."

Melanie noticed her father's dejected expression and decided to lighten the atmosphere a little. "Since when was your grandfather a horse thief?" she asked Caleb.

"Not my grandfather, hers. And he wasn't a horse thief, he was just hanged for one. And he didn't die, because the guys doing the hanging, who were his brothers, by the way, were drunk. They threw the lynch rope over a thin, dead branch, and it snapped. Which was good, because the next day they realized the horse they thought he'd stolen was his own."

Seeing her father chuckle, Melanie thought about kissing Caleb right then and there. Instead, she shook her head. "I know you have a colorful family, but I don't believe a word of it."

"It's true." Caleb held up his right hand, palm out. "I swear."

Melanie turned to her father. "Are you buying any of this?"

"Why not? After a night like this, I'd believe just about anything."

"It has been a hell of a night," Fayrene agreed.

"Well, I'll tell you all right here and now," Ralph said. "I'm through with gambling. I've learned my lesson."

"That's good," Melanie said, "because that money I paid him is the last that will ever leave the PR coffers to pay off a gambling debt. I mean it, Daddy, not another penny, not ever again."

Fayrene bristled. "Don't you talk to your father that way. You be nice to him."

Thinking to leave the room and give the family their first privacy of the night, Caleb straightened from where he'd been leaning against the counter and took a step across the floor. "I'll just—"

Melanie put a hand on his chest. "Stay put, coward. We don't have a single secret left from you anyway." Then she turned to her mother. "You're a fine one to talk. He's your husband and you don't even live with him."

"How do you know I'm not changing my mind about that?"

The look of hope that sprang to her father's face brought tears to Melanie's eyes.

"Are you?" Ralph asked. "Do you mean it? Are you coming home?"

Fayrene propped her hands on her hips and thrust out her chest. Like steel filings to a magnet, Ralph's gaze zeroed in. Fayrene smiled. "Under two conditions."

Ralph swallowed, but his eyes were locked on the piping outlining the yoke of her shirt. "Just name them."

"Number one, no more gambling. Not a single penny. Whatever you've got down on next weekend's OU–Texas football game, you can forget."

Ralph had the good grace to blush. He had, indeed, already placed a bet on the game. Still, he nodded. "Done."

"I mean it, Ralphie. You go gambling again and I'm gone, for good this time."

"You got it. You said two conditions. What's the second?"

"That you don't ignore me the way you used to."

Ralph blinked in surprise. "Ignore you?"

"By working all hours of the day and night, dragging in way past dark, so tired you can't hold your eyes open, let alone have a conversation. I'm your wife, and I want some of your time and attention. I want you to talk to me, watch a TV show with me now and then, maybe even go out to a movie or something. I want to be treated like a wife, not a live-in housekeeper."

Ralph swallowed. "I guess you're going to have to help me out on that. Remind me when I'm slipping up."

"You can be sure I will. And the first thing you're going to have to do is hire more help around this place so you don't work yourself into an early grave. I'm way too young to be a widow."

Melanie felt the need to butt in. "Mama, there's no

money to hire back the men we usually have, much less extra help.''

"It's really that bad?" Fayrene asked. "I can't believe that.''

"Believe it. I still haven't figured out how we're going to pay for Lucy and Ethel.''

"Who?" Ralph asked.

"Never mind," Melanie said. "What I mean is, we're broke.''

Caleb stepped forward. "If you're going to make me stay for this conversation, then I get to contribute to it.''

"Go ahead," Ralph told him. "Like she said, after tonight we sure don't have any secrets from you.''

"You should take on a partner.''

"A partner?" He said it as though Caleb had suggested he grow an extra head.

"Someone to buy a share of the ranch for cash, and who would take part of the day-to-day workload off your shoulders. That solves two of your problems right there—cash, and more time to spend, uh, doing whatever.''

Ralph was already shaking his head before Caleb finished. "I'm not about to let some stranger buy part of the PR, come in here and tell me how to run my own ranch.''

"No, I didn't mean it like that. You wouldn't want to sell a controlling share. You wouldn't want him to have a share larger than yours. Melanie owns half the ranch, doesn't she?''

Fayrene blinked. "We really don't have any secrets.''

"Ah, come on, Miz Pruitt, you know how close Melanie and I have always been. It's not like she blabs everything to everybody, but she talks to me. But she owns half, and the two of you have a fourth each. You could leave Mel with her half, then take the other half, that right now is split in two, and split it in thirds, instead. Or any other way you wanted to split it.''

Ralph crossed his arms. ''Hmmph. Who would want to go along with a deal like that, buy into a broke ranch, then work it, to boot?''

''What about me?'' Caleb offered. God help him, Ralph had just given up gambling, and Caleb was taking the biggest gamble of his life with this offer.

''You?'' Melanie asked, puzzled.

''Why you?'' Ralph asked, sharing a quick look with his wife.

''Because,'' Caleb said, his heart thundering against his ribs, ''I don't figure Melanie will want to live on the Cherokee Rose after we're married, so I'll need to live here. As for the work, I have to have something to do all day, right?''

''Married?'' Ralph asked, skepticism plain on his face.

''Married?'' Fayrene's face lit with hope.

''Married?'' Melanie shrieked. ''Who says we're getting married?''

''I do. You said you love me. I love you, too. Marriage is the next logical step, right?''

''If that's a marriage proposal,'' she said heatedly, ''it's the dumbest one I've ever heard. I know you haven't been kicked in the head lately. Maybe aliens came down from space and took over your body, because I don't know you.''

Caleb sauntered over toward her. ''Sure you do. I'm that other brother. Your best friend. I can't do the bended-knee thing and give you a proper proposal because that would mean I was treating you differently from when we were just friends, and you said you didn't want that.''

The fluttering in Melanie's stomach rose up to tickle the inside of her throat. Her hands shook, so she clasped them behind her back. ''Maybe I'd make an exception. For this, I mean.''

If she laughed in his face and made a joke of it all, Caleb didn't know what he'd do. But the look in her eyes, the fear tinged with a touch of what looked like hope, had him taking a deep breath and dropping to one knee.

''Melanie, will you marry me and be my best friend, my lover, my partner, for the rest of our lives?''

A tiny cry escaped before she clamped a hand over her mouth. Her eyes filled with moisture. She blinked rapidly so she could see him clearly. She wanted to remember this moment for the rest of her life.

''Well?'' he demanded, growing concerned when she didn't answer.

Melanie threw her arms wide and fell against him. ''I thought you'd never ask!''

Caleb squeezed his eyes shut and held on to her for all he was worth. Damned if he would ever let her go.

''Did you hear that, Ralph? Oh, my. Our baby's going to marry Caleb.''

''How about that,'' Ralph answered. ''How about that.''

Caleb heard them say something else, but he couldn't make out the words over the pounding of his own heart. Something about somebody named Lucy and somebody else named Ethel, but since he didn't know anyone by those names, he let it go.

"I love you," he whispered to the woman in his arms. "I love you."

"Oh, Caleb, I love you, too. Are we crazy?"

"Probably." They rose with their arms around each other and he held her tight. "But who cares?"

"Surely," she said, kissing his neck, his jaw, his cheek. "Surely somebody somewhere does."

Caleb threaded his fingers into her hair and angled her mouth toward his. "To hell with them." He took her mouth with his and drank deep and long. A need rose up in him, sharp and strong. He fed it, fed on her. She was his. She'd said yes. He still couldn't believe it. Could he be dreaming?

He prayed not. Prayed that he was awake and this was real and they were really getting married.

"I want you," he murmured against her mouth.

"Yes." She sounded as breathless as he was. "Yes."

He tore his mouth from hers and buried his face against her hair. "We're in your kitchen."

Melanie pulled back and blinked. "Oh. Yeah."

"We've got a problem," he told her.

She nudged her hips against his, putting pressure on his erection, and smiled slyly. "I'd take care of that for you, but as you say, we're in the kitchen."

"And your parents are home. But our main problem is, neither one of us ever left the damn nest."

"Ah." She didn't need it spelled out. "I live with my parents, you live with your family."

"I'm going to be taking a lot of cold showers between now and the time we're married."

She leaned up and rubbed her smooth cheek against his raspy one. "We'll find a way. I promise."

"A quick wedding date would solve the problem.

After that, I'll just have to get used to making love to you down the hall from your parents.''

Melanie chuckled. ''I think for the next little while my parents are going to so preoccupied with each other that they'll never notice.''

Chapter Ten

It should have been a relatively simple matter, Caleb thought, to set a date, make arrangements, get married. It wasn't the invasion of Normandy, for crying out loud, it was just a wedding. His wedding, Caleb acknowledged, and he wanted it done.

But that contrary woman he'd proposed to and who had accepted could think up more delaying tactics than fleas on a hound.

First, she and her parents needed a few days together as a family. After her mother's two-year absence and her father's recent disastrous gambling streak, Caleb was forced to agree a little family time for the three of them was surely called for. He couldn't begrudge them a few days. A week.

Then she had to help her dad hire new men and spend a few days getting them acquainted with the PR and how things were done there.

Okay, Caleb could buy that. How could a woman think about picking a wedding date when she had all that on her mind?

Events at his home weren't helping anything, either. It took nearly a week to get one group of the Mexicans settled in New Mexico with family members who had immigrated years earlier. Then they made arrangements for some to go to Texas where they said they had friends.

Most of the rest of the group decided to go to Tennessee where they heard that a food-processing plant didn't care if their workers were illegal. They paid what to an American would be slave wages, but to the Mexicans was decent money for plucking and cutting up chickens.

That left only Pedro, Maria and little Rosa. They would have been gone by now, but Pedro had made himself practically indispensable taking up some of the slack caused by Caleb spending so much time at the PR of late.

Melanie might be having trouble deciding on a wedding date, but Ralph seemed downright eager to settle the details of the new partnership. They had decided that Melanie would, indeed, keep her fifty percent. Fayrene, Ralph and Caleb would split the remaining fifty percent equally among them, giving them each one-sixth of the Pruitt Ranch. When it came to ranch business, Melanie's decisions would be final unless the other three partners agreed on a different course of action. Then they'd be tied, fifty-fifty, and nothing would get done, but what the hell. The point was that the ranch would always belong to Melanie. Caleb had no quarrel with that. He would work his fingers to nubs to make the ranch prosper for her and their children.

Children. There was another topic Melanie hadn't found the time to discuss. She had always said she wanted children, so he didn't know what the big deal was. If he could ever get her alone for five damn minutes, maybe he'd ask her about it.

But then, who was he kidding? If he got her alone for five damn minutes he wasn't going to want to talk about anything. He was going to want to jump her bones.

"You look like you're a thousand miles away."

Caleb jerked away from the corral fence involuntarily as if shot. He hadn't heard Sloan come up behind him.

"But I guess you're just over on the next ranch." Sloan punched him on the upper arm and chuckled.

"Actually," Caleb said, "I was wondering how Earline's enjoying her retirement." It wasn't a complete lie. He'd been thinking about Earline about an hour ago. Thinking how odd it was to walk into the house and find Maria doing all the things Earline used to do. The cooking, the cleaning, the general taking care of the house and family.

Earline had been keeping house for the Chisholms for more years than Caleb could remember. That she would finally retire to enjoy her golden years at home with her husband and all the grandchildren who lived near them shouldn't have come as a surprise. But Earline had seen in Maria someone capable, eager, and in dire need of a home and job.

Earline's recommendation alone would have been enough to guarantee Maria the job, considering how much Rose liked the young woman. But Pedro was equally well liked by Sloan and Justin.

Caleb hadn't spent as much time with the man as

his brothers had, but from what he'd seen, the Cherokee Rose would benefit from his presence. He wasn't a rancher, but he was an excellent caretaker of buildings, equipment and animals. He could do all those pesky things Caleb and his brothers kept putting off because they couldn't be done from the back of a horse.

And they were going to need an extra full-time person once Caleb made the move to the PR.

"If you ask me," Sloan said, "she was just waiting for someone like Maria to come along so she could retire. She might have retired when she met Emily, but Emily made it plain that she wasn't after her job."

"Speaking of Emily," Caleb said, "how is married life these days?"

Sloan chuckled. "Contemplating your future, are you?"

Caleb shrugged and turned back to watch Sloan's new mare prance around the corral.

"Getting cold feet?" Sloan asked quietly.

"Hell, no," Caleb said forcefully. "Not me."

"Melanie, then."

"What makes you say that?"

"Because it's been two weeks and the two of you haven't set a date yet." And because he knew his brother and didn't want to see him brood, he asked, "Are you really going to like living with her parents?"

Caleb's lips twitched. "Probably not. How do you think Emily likes living with all of us?"

"I'll admit I was concerned about that at first."

"Not anymore?"

Sloan shook his head and propped his boot next to Caleb's on the fence rail. "Emily never had a family. As far as she's concerned, the more people in this house the better she likes it."

"What about you?" Caleb asked. "Wouldn't you like a little privacy for the two of you now and then?"

"Not really. The honeymoon was great, don't get me wrong. We did need that, and probably will again, maybe on a regular basis. But no matter how much we enjoyed our time alone together, we were both glad to get home. There's a lot to be said for being surrounded by family."

"Yeah, but all the time?"

Sloan laughed. "There's always the lock on the bedroom door. And when we use it, we're lucky enough to have somebody else in the house to look after the girls for us. If it was just us, Emily and me and the girls, our privacy would be even more scarce."

"Melanie and I won't have children to worry about. Not right off, anyway."

"Oh, I don't know. From what I hear, Fayrene and Ralph have been acting like a couple of teenagers in heat. They probably qualify as children."

"Man." Caleb shook his head and laughed. "Poor Ralph can't keep his eyes off her. Or his hands, I imagine. He just about drools over that new chest of hers."

Sloan shook his head. "Why'd she go and do that to herself? I mean, she looks great, but there was nothing wrong with her before."

"She says she did it to get Ralph's attention."

"I'd say it worked."

"She got her money's worth, that's for sure."

"Is Mel still dragging her feet about a wedding date?" Sloan asked quietly.

Caleb let out a harsh breath. "Yeah. That sure seems to be what she's doing, even though she denies it."

"Have patience, bro. She's just a little scared, that's all."

"I've figured that much out for myself. Every time I try to get her to talk about it she finds a way to dodge the subject. What I'm not sure of is what she's afraid of. Me? Marriage? Marriage to me?" He shook his head.

Sloan worried that he might be betraying a confidence, but Emily had not asked him to keep it a secret, hadn't mentioned Mel extracting any promise of secrecy from her. Caleb was his brother. He loved Melanie like a sister, but his loyalty went first to Caleb. Until the two of them married, he thought with a smile, then all bets were off.

For now, however, he couldn't leave Caleb stumbling around in the dark if he had the means to shed a little light. He leaned his elbows on the top rail and watched his new mare.

"And here I thought you were the one who knew her the best," he offered lazily. "She's scared of herself. Unsure of herself."

"I suspected as much, but I can't get a handle on it. And Lord knows she won't talk about it."

"She thinks she's, I don't know, fickle or something. She figured out she didn't really love me, and every man she's been interested in since, she's gotten bored with after a few weeks. She thinks that's all she's able to do. I imagine she's afraid what she's feeling for you won't last."

"She's told me something similar. But she's wrong. She's got the biggest heart, and no one on earth is more steadfast."

"I know that, and you know that. You've just got to find a way to make her see it."

"Ha. Is that all? Get Melanie to change her mind about something?"

"You got her to change her mind about just being friends, didn't you?"

"Yeah." Caleb perked up. "I did, didn't I."

"So maybe you're not as useless as I've always thought you were."

"Hey, I resemble that statement."

At the PR, Melanie wasn't as amenable to advice as Caleb had been. She wished heartily that no one knew she and Caleb had agreed to marry.

Why did everyone want to talk about it all the damn time? First her mother, then her father, then her mother again. She was only glad there wasn't anyone else around except two new hands who didn't know her well enough to open their mouths to her about anything personal.

There must be a chart somewhere, she decided, that told her parents whose turn it was to corner her and oh so casually pressure her to set a wedding date. Pink square for Mama's turn, blue square for Daddy. This evening must have been a blue square. He found her in the barn with their three boarder mares.

"No," she said before he could open his mouth. "We have not set a date yet."

"Did I say anything?" he cried. "I didn't say anything. You've just got a guilty conscience, that's all."

"What do I have to feel guilty about?"

Her father shook his head. "From a female point of view, probably nothing."

"What's that mean, female point of view?"

"You women just live to make a man dance to your tune. Promise a man you'll do something he wants real bad, then hold out as long as possible and make him sweat, just for the fun of it, before you finally make good on it."

Melanie paused before turning away toward the tack room. This wasn't about her. "This is about you and Mama, isn't it? She promised you something and now she's putting you off."

"Damn woman."

"You're crazy in love with that damn woman."

He stomped away three paces, then back again, his arms flapping at his sides. "Of course I am. Always have been. What's that got to do with anything?"

"How did you know, Daddy? All those years ago, how did you know she was the one, that you two would stay together, that it would work out between you?"

"Work out? You call this working out? She's driving me crazy."

"Maybe, but she's here, isn't she? And you still love each other."

"For all the good that does."

Melanie snorted. "And you want to know why I won't pick a date to get married?"

"Ah, hell, little girl, forget I said anything. Just because I'm miserable doesn't mean you will be."

Didn't it? She had to wonder. "What did Mama promise that she won't deliver on?" Then she held out a hand. "If it has anything to do with sex forget I asked." Logically, she knew her parents were two warm-blooded people who adored each other. She couldn't help it, however, if it seemed weird to her to know they were having sex.

Having sex, hell. They appeared to have been going at it like a couple of bunny rabbits since her mother's return, if the number of times her father disappeared into the house each day was anything to go by.

"No." He laughed. "It's nothing that private. It's

just that she keeps stalling about sending for her things in Phoenix.''

"Why would she stall? She's already said she's home to stay.''

"My thoughts exactly," he said with a sharp nod. "But if she won't send for her things, maybe she's thinking she might not stay after all."

And it hurt him. It was easy to see in his eyes now that she knew what was going on. Her mother's uncertainty was tearing her father apart.

"Oh, Daddy." She slipped an arm around his waist and put her head on his shoulder. "I'm sorry. I'm sure she doesn't mean it like that. Maybe she's just scared."

"She doesn't trust me, that's what it is. I promised I wouldn't gamble or take her for granted anymore, but I've given her no reason to trust me in the past."

"I'm sure that's not it, Daddy. Maybe it's herself she's not sure of. She gave up on us before. Maybe she's afraid she doesn't...oh my God." It all came clear to her, like a heavy fog suddenly lifting to reveal a sharp, clear landscape.

"What? What's wrong, Mel?"

She shook her head and looked at her father. "Nothing. I just think maybe she's afraid she doesn't have what it takes to stick it out if everything doesn't go smoothly in the future. Maybe she's afraid she's the one who'll fail."

The way I'm afraid, she thought with new clarity.

It wasn't setting a date that scared her, or even marrying Caleb. What scared her was her own lousy track record with relationships. With the exception of chasing after Sloan all her life, she had never stuck with anyone for any length of time. She never let anyone get close. She never tried to get close to anyone.

Until Caleb. Even then, it wasn't as if she had *let* him get close. He'd more or less barged his way into her heart and planted himself there. And now that he'd gone and made her fall in love with him, he thought they should get married. He'd asked, she'd said yes. And had dragged her feet in the two weeks since.

Was she hurting him the way her mother was hurting her father? Was Caleb making excuses for her the way her father was for her mother?

She searched her heart for answers but could find only one: yes. Yes, she was hurting him, and yes, he was probably making excuses for her behavior.

But there was another question, a harder one to answer. What was she going to do now? She couldn't expect him to wait around forever for her to make up her mind. After all, she had told him she would marry him. She *wanted* to marry him. Didn't she? She loved him, wanted no other man but him, wanted to spend the rest of her life with him.

But, maybe like her mother, she feared she didn't have what it took to make a marriage work.

What she had to do now was make up her mind. She could set a date and pray like crazy that she didn't screw up Caleb's life by marrying him, or she could call it off and maybe, if she was very, very lucky, be his friend again.

Who was she kidding? Why would he ever want to be her friend again if she turned her back on him now? She had to marry him or let him go. There could be no in-between.

Later that evening Caleb stood before the mirror in his room and gave himself the once-over. Twice. Clean shirt and jeans, boots shined. Hair combed. Freshly shaved.

He would have to do. He rushed down the stairs and toward the door. "I'm going out," he called. "Don't wait up."

Behind him, his grandmother, sister-in-law and two brothers shared a look and a knowing smile.

"Give our best to Melanie," Rose said.

Caleb didn't bother replying. There was no such thing as a secret in this house, he thought. But then, any idiot could have figured out where he was going, if the smell of his new aftershave was any indication.

Had he overdone the aftershave?

Hell with it. It was too late now, in any case. He jumped into his pickup and barreled down the driveway. He was a man on a mission.

He hadn't called Melanie to tell her he was coming or ask if she was available. He didn't want to take the chance that she might come up with an excuse to put him off. She hadn't done that yet, but whenever they saw each other she seemed to be holding her breath to see what he wanted to talk about. Or she would start rambling about something that had nothing to do with anything, talking so fast that he couldn't get a word in.

Not tonight. Tonight they were going to get to the bottom of the situation. If he was going to lose her, he would just as soon find out now.

Tough talk, he thought, for a guy crazy in love with a reluctant woman.

It was that reluctance he had to find a way to surmount. He didn't know how he was going to do that, but he would think of something. He had to. He didn't intend to spend the rest of his life without her.

* * *

Melanie gave herself a final once-over in the mirror above her dresser. She had looked better in her day, but an hour ago she had looked decidedly worse. Caleb knew her in all her looks, so she doubted her appearance would make much difference, but, as her mother had drilled into her head her entire life, it never hurts to look your best.

"Listen to me," she muttered to her reflection. "Taking grooming advice from someone with fake boobs." She shook her head. She would not fault her mother for getting breast implants. If implants made her mother happy, then power to her. To Melanie such things were nonsense. But then, she was pushing twenty-nine and had never been married, so that showed what she knew about getting what she wanted from a man.

Go figure.

What she wanted from Caleb, he couldn't give her, but she owed it to him to be honest.

She was thinking about him so much, so hard, that when she stepped out the back door with her keys in hand, on her way to drive to the Rose to see him, and there he stood, on her sidewalk in the waning evening light, she thought she had conjured him up out of thin air.

"Hi," he said. "Going somewhere?"

Honesty. Wasn't that her goal? "I was on my way to see you."

"You were?" He cocked his head to one side. "What for?"

"Can't a girl come visit her guy without having to give a reason?"

He took her hand and brought it to his lips. "This

girl can come see this guy whenever she wants." He kissed the back of her hand. "For any reason on earth, or no reason at all."

Melanie batted her lashes. "Why, Caleb Chisholm, I had no idea you were such a sweet-talking devil."

He pulled her close and wrapped his arms around her. "I've missed you."

She started to laugh and remind him that it had only been two days since they'd seen each other. Instead, she laid her head on his shoulder and sighed. "I've missed you, too."

With a finger beneath her chin, he tilted her face up toward him. "Have you?"

A lump rose in Melanie's throat. If he had to ask, then she'd been right earlier—she had hurt him. "Oh, Caleb, I'm so sorry you feel the need to ask that."

"Shh," he whispered. "It's all right."

"No, it's not."

He smiled slightly. "Wanna fight about it?"

She tucked her head beneath his chin again. "No."

"Come for a ride with me."

"Okay."

"If you're hungry we can go to town and I'll buy you a burger."

"Okay."

"I'll bring you home whenever you say."

She pulled back and looked at him. "I said okay."

"Oh. Okay. Let's go, then."

"Let me tell Mama and Daddy so they won't wonder what happened to me." She ran back and stuck her head in the door, telling her parents she was leaving with Caleb and not to wait up. As if they would, she thought with a silent laugh.

"You two have a good time," her father called.

"And set a wedding date," came her mother's demand.

Melanie cringed, hoping Caleb hadn't heard the latter. She wasn't ready for that conversation yet. Maybe that hamburger he promised would give her courage.

On the ride into town Melanie scooted over and sat pressed against Caleb's side. She had a need to touch him, to feel him next to her as much as possible.

Caleb welcomed the warmth, both physical and emotional, of her nearness. Until she told him differently, they were still engaged to be married. That implied a certain level of intimacy, such as a man being able to rest his arm along his woman's thigh, his hand just above her knee.

It felt good to touch her. Felt even better when she placed her hand on top of his and threaded her fingers with his.

This was something new for Melanie. She didn't usually touch him in such a casual yet intimate way as holding hands. If he took her hand in his, that was one thing. But for her to make the move…it made his heart pound.

By the time they made the city limits of Rose Rock the sky was dark, the stars starting to pop out.

"What'll it be?" Caleb asked. "Hamburger, chili dog or pizza? Or we could hit the café for a steak or something."

"I'll go with your original offer of a burger."

"A burger it is." He drove down Main to the hamburger stand and pulled in and parked. They got out together and placed their order at the walk-up window, then sat at one of the nearby picnic tables. The temperature was holding in the midsixties, so it was comfortable where they sat beneath the awning. They watched the cars drive by and waited for their order to be called. They didn't talk much.

Caleb had plenty he wanted to say to her, but he got the impression Melanie had things to tell him, too, but that she wasn't ready. It was hard for him not to push her. Still, he managed to bide his time. Whatever they ended up saying to each other tonight would be better said when they were alone. Here there were too many people coming and going, walking over to say hello, yelling out from their cars as they drove by.

He could wait a little longer. They would eat first, then find someplace private. Then, they would talk.

The problem was, even then they didn't talk. After they finished their burgers they drove to the river a few miles outside of town. Caleb found a private place to park beneath the blackjacks and cottonwoods along the bank. He killed the lights, the engine, the radio, and they sat quietly, Melanie snug against his side with her head on his shoulder, their joined hands on her leg, and listened to the frogs and the rustling leaves and the river.

Caleb decided she was never going to speak. He would have to dive in and brave the waters. Then she surprised him by speaking first.

"I'm afraid, Caleb."

He pulled her into his arms, turning her to face him, putting her back to the steering wheel. "I know you are. What are you afraid of?"

She lowered her gaze and centered it somewhere in the vicinity of his chin. "Of messing everything up. I'm so afraid of messing things up that I mess up trying not to mess up."

"You know, I hate to admit it, but I actually understood that. I think."

Melanie pinched his arm.

"Ouch!" He rubbed the sore spot. "What was that for?"

"I'm being serious and you're making fun of me."

"I'm being serious. But you're wrong, you know. As far as I can tell, you haven't messed up anything at all."

"I've messed up something pretty good if you have to ask whether or not I've missed you."

Caleb shook his head. "That's just your self-defense mechanism working overtime. You think I don't know that?"

"I wish you'd have told me. I'm just barely figuring it out for myself. I've hurt your feelings by not settling on a date."

What could he say to that? She had him there. "Have you figured out why you're not ready to set a date?"

"I don't know." She shrugged and lowered her gaze. "I guess I'm afraid we'll get married and then you'll figure out I'm a fake and it'll be too late and we'll have to turn around and get a divorce."

"There you go again, building up another disaster in your head." He managed a small laugh.

"Yeah, I know. Dumb, isn't it?"

"It's not dumb if it's something that scares you. But if you're going in the door thinking divorce is just ahead, then it'll never work. Why bother making the commitment if you've already got your escape route planned? There's no need to even try to make things work if you've got one foot out the door before we start. If I could give you a guarantee that everything would be easy, Melanie, I would. I'd write it in my own blood if it would reassure you.''

''No,'' she whispered, pressing her fingers over his lips. ''No. This problem is in me, not you. I know there are no guarantees. I know that. I just need to stop being afraid, and I don't know how to do that.''

''You need to believe in yourself, and I don't know how to help you do that. In every other part of your life you don't have a doubt in the world about who you are and what you want or where your place is in everything. I don't understand why this, us, you and me, is any different, but I know for you it is. All I ask is that you be honest with me, tell me what's going on. If you're unsure or afraid or angry or anything, tell me. I might not be able to help, but I want to know. Need to know.''

Melanie trembled at his words and the depth of meaning behind then. He wasn't asking for mere words. He was asking her to make herself vulnerable to him.

Let me in. That's what he'd said the day they'd made love. That's what he was asking now. That she let him in. Inside her heart, her head.

Did she have the courage to open herself to him that way, make herself completely vulnerable to him? Give him that kind of power over her again, only more so this time?

''Why does the thought of being honest with me scare you so much?''

''Who says I'm scared?''

''Hell, you should see your face. You can't hide it from me. I don't understand why you think you need to try. You're an honest person. It's not like you make a career out of lying. Talk to me, dammit.''

"What do you want me to say?" She threw herself across the cab to the passenger's side. "That you're the one person in the world who can hurt me? Is that what you want to hear? That if I don't protect myself from you you'll be able to tear me apart?"

He turned sideways and leaned toward her. "My God, Melanie, what is it you think I'm going to do to you?"

"See?" she cried, panic seizing her throat. "You tell me to talk to you, to be honest about what scares me, and when I am, you don't want to hear it."

Somewhere in the back of her mind she knew she was being irrational, she simply couldn't stop herself. All her thoughts and fears and outrageous hopes swirled inside her in ever-tightening circles until she feared she might implode.

"I notice," Caleb said after a long moment, "that you didn't answer my question."

Her breath came in fast little pants. "Take me home."

More than stunned, Caleb leaned back against the driver's door and stared at her. He'd never seen her like this. She was like a wolf caught in a trap, trying to gnaw off its own foot to get free. And he couldn't bear to see her suffer this way.

"All right," he said, his dreams turning bitter on his tongue. "All right, Melanie, you win. I'll take you home."

Chapter Eleven

"Holy smokes!" Ralph gaped at his daughter the next morning across the breakfast table. "What the devil happened to you? You look like you've been rode hard and put up wet."

"Ralph!" Fayrene scolded. "What a thing to say to your own daughter. Comparing her to a horse. Although," she added, giving Melanie a closer look, "you do look a little rough around the edges this morning, baby. What's wrong?"

Rough around the edges, Melanie thought, was putting it mildly. She'd seen herself in the mirror. Her face was blotchy, her eyes swollen, her lips puffy. She looked as if she'd been crying all night. Probably because she had been.

"I didn't sleep much," she said to her mother. "I might be coming down with a cold."

Fayrene pursed her lips a moment, then said, "If you

say so. If you ask me, you're complicating this whole marriage thing way too much.''

Melanie blinked her swollen, gritty eyes. "What?"

Fayrene stood next to Melanie's chair and smoothed a hand down her daughter's hair. "I know you, baby. You're worrying too much. It's only prewedding jitters, that's all.''

Melanie sniffed. "It's just a cold."

"You're just a little nervous at the thought of suddenly sharing your life with another person. But this other person, baby, is Caleb, and he adores you. All you have to remember is that when you love somebody, you want that person to be happy. You,'' she said, pointing a long, manicured nail at Melanie, "love Caleb. You want him to be happy. You are the only person he'll ever be happy with. It's simple, see? Marrying him will make both of you happy.''

"As happy as a couple of clams," Ralph chimed in.

Melanie sneered. "Clams don't get happy, they get steamed. Then they get eaten and disappear. They no longer exist.''

"Oh, baby." Fayrene smoothed Melanie's hair back again. "Is that what you think is going to happen to you? No wonder you won't settle on a wedding date.''

"No, Mama, I was just running off at the mouth. I don't think I'll disappear if I marry Caleb.''

"Whew. That's good. For a minute there…" Then Fayrene laughed. "But how silly of me. Of course you're not calling off the wedding.''

Melanie swallowed. Technically, her mother was absolutely correct. Melanie was not calling off the wedding. Caleb had pretty much taken care of that last night. At least, it seemed that way to her.

Of course, last night had been a complete disaster

all the way around. She had ruined everything. She had tried to do what she thought was right, what he had asked of her. She'd tried to be honest and explain her emotions, her fear. But in doing so she had hurt him deeply. Maybe even angered him. Surely insulted him.

After all of that, there had been no need for her to call off the wedding. She had asked him to take her home, but his answer, when he'd said that she had won, had been about much more than her request to go home. He had given up. On her, on them.

"No, Mama," she said. "I'm not calling off the wedding, but I'm afraid Caleb might."

"Don't be ridiculous," her mother cried. "That boy is crazy in love with you."

"I know he is."

"And you're crazy in love with him. Any fool can see that."

Melanie nodded without speaking. "But I hurt his feelings last night."

"So?" her father said. "Apologize. Kiss and make up. Hell, making up is some of the most fun there is in life."

Apologize. Could it possibly be that simple? Melanie didn't see how. An apology wouldn't keep her irrational fear from turning her into a raving lunatic again.

"I don't mean to sound harsh, baby," her mother said. "But it seems to me you need to make up your mind once and for all. That's a fine man you've hooked up with. You need to either marry him or cut him loose."

Cut him loose? The words jarred Melanie. She felt as if someone had just jerked her chair from beneath her and left her hanging in midair. Like the coyote racing off the edge of a cliff into midair. Then he looks down, realizes the ground is gone, and plunges.

Of course, after he crashed to earth he picked himself up and carried on. You could do that in cartoons. In real life, things were different. The ground was much less forgiving.

"A man like Caleb," her mother went on, "needs a wife and family of his own. And he's not getting any younger. If you're not going to marry him, let him go so he can find somebody else to marry and spend the rest of his life with."

Somebody else? Caleb, married to someone else? Melanie couldn't conceive of it. But what else could she expect? He had proven to her last night that he wasn't going to put up with being hurt and insulted and neglected for long.

Dear God, what had she done with all her waffling, her whining, her stupid fears?

"I've got to go." She jumped from her chair, grabbed her keys from their peg by the back door and dashed out.

In the quiet wake of her leaving, Ralph chuckled. "Cut him loose? So he can find somebody else? Oh, Mama, you're a mean one."

"Well, it's past time somebody gave her a shove. She's dillydallying too much for my taste. I want a wedding. Grandbabies. We leave it up to her, it'll be years before we get either."

The sun was barely up when Melanie tore up the gravel driveway at the Cherokee Rose and skidded to a stop in front of the barn. Rose and her grandsons should be pouring out of the house any minute and heading out to work for the day.

Sure enough, just as she climbed out of her rig and started across toward the side door of the house, that door opened. But it wasn't Caleb who came out, it was Sloan.

He was on the third step down from the porch to the sidewalk before he spotted her. He drew up short.

"Mel. What are you doing here this early?"

"I need to talk with Caleb. Thought I'd better catch him before he headed out for the day."

"Good idea. And yes," Sloan said darkly, "I think you do need to talk to him. He thinks the two of you are doomed, that you don't love him enough to marry him."

A huge, painful lump rose in Melanie's throat. "He said that?"

"He didn't have to. It was written all over his face when he came home last night. Came home much too damn early for having spent the evening with the woman he's getting ready to marry."

"Look, Sloan, this is between Caleb and me. I appreciate your concern, but—"

"Oh no you don't. Don't you dare tell me to butt out. Not after the way you stuck your nose in last summer with Emily and me."

"You needed it."

"I did. Yes."

"You were being pigheaded."

"You're right, I was."

"It's different with Caleb and me."

"I'm sure it is," Sloan admitted. "I'm not sure what's going on. I don't think I need to know. I just want to remind you that you've looked all your life for a man to love you the way he does. I'm sorry it couldn't have been me, but that's behind us. No one knows the two of you better than I do and I'm telling you that you and Caleb belong together. So whatever this trouble is, fix it.''

"Fix it? That's you're great advice?''

"It'll do. Fix it, kiss and make up, get married. You'll never regret it, Mel. You won't find a man better than him and you know it.''

"Dammit, I'm not looking for a man better than him.''

"That's a relief to know.''

At the sound of Caleb's voice behind her, Melanie gasped and whirled. "Where did you come from?''

"I was in the tack room. I thought I heard someone drive up.''

He looked so good to her in the early-morning light. In any light. "I'm sorry,'' she said.

Caleb cocked his head to one side. "For what?''

He wasn't going to make this easy. Fair enough. She didn't deserve easy. "I'm sorry…'' She peered out the corner of her eye. "I'm sorry that we don't seem to have any privacy.''

Sloan tossed his hands in the air. "All right, all right. Sheesh. I'm going.''

"Let's walk,'' Caleb said. He turned and headed toward the creek beyond the house.

Melanie followed, not sure what to make of the lack of emotion in his voice and on his face. Then again, she'd known facing him wouldn't be easy.

Beside an old cottonwood at the edge of the creek, Caleb stopped and turned toward her. "I admit I'm surprised to see you.''

"I guess you would be, after last night. Caleb, I hurt you last night, and that's the last thing I ever want to do. I'm so sorry.''

"I asked for honesty, you gave it to me. You're afraid I'm going to hurt you, so you're keeping me at arm's length."

Melanie crossed her arms and glanced back toward the barn and corrals. "That's pretty much what I said. Dumb, huh?"

"Not to you it isn't."

"Dammit, Caleb, stop it," she cried.

"Stop what?"

"Stop being so damn nice, so understanding. What, are you bucking for sainthood? Saint Caleb, so understanding. Or maybe it's martyrdom. Maybe that's what you're after. Just let me walk all over you. Stand by your woman no matter how much of a bitch she turns in to."

"Pardon?" This, Caleb thought with a tingling along his spine, did not sound like a woman afraid of being hurt.

"Pardon," she mimicked. "Don't go all sarcastic on me. I didn't mean to hurt you last night. I haven't meant to hurt you however many times I've hurt you in the past couple of weeks. I'd rather cut off my right arm than hurt you."

When he didn't say anything, she started pacing back and forth in front of him, waving her arms wildly in the air.

"I've been a basket case, all right? Out of my mind trying to figure out if this marriage thing can possibly work. Not for me," she added with a wave of her arm. "Hell, all I have to do is get within ten feet of you and I'm happy. But I figure you might want a little something more than that from me, and I'm not sure I know what that is."

"Okay, hold it." Caleb held a hand up to stop her.

"You think I want something you can't give, and that scares you. You think I'm going to hurt you, and that scares you. Have I got this much right?"

Wary of his dark tone, she nodded. "That's right."

"Then what," he asked tightly, "are you doing here? Why are we even having this conversation? Why haven't we just gone our separate ways?"

"Is that what you want? For us to go our separate ways?"

"Of course it's not," he offered earnestly. "But if you think I'm going to stand around and be the cause of you tearing yourself to pieces out of fear of what might or might not happen, then guess again."

"Would you listen to the two of us?" Melanie scrubbed both hands up and down her face, then dropped her arms to her sides and faced him. "We're both out of our minds. When we were friends we never even argued. No strife, no stress, no tension. Just friendship. Somebody to count on."

"You don't think you can count on me anymore?"

Her small smile nearly broke his heart. "Of course I can count on you. Always. You told me so, and I believed you."

"Do you want to go back to being friends again?"

"You mean just friends?"

"Yes." If she agreed, it would kill him.

She shook her head. "It's way too late for that, Caleb. I do want us to be friends, but we can't be *just* friends when we love each other this much."

Caleb felt his heart simply stop. Then it started again with a hard thud against his ribs. "Then what is it you do want?"

"I want to feel like a sane person again, and the only way I can do that is if you help me. I love you,

Caleb. Right now I'm a little bit wacky. I'm hoping that'll pass, but if it doesn't, then you're stuck with a crazy woman. If you think you can't handle that, then just say so.''

Caleb placed his hands on the balls of her shoulders. ''If I knew what to do so you wouldn't be afraid, I'd do it in a heartbeat.''

''Then marry me.''

''What?'' He stared, dumbfounded.

''A week from Saturday. If the church isn't available, we'll try the VFW hall, or the rec center, or the barn for all I care. Just marry me.''

A slow smile spread across Caleb's mouth as the weight of the past two weeks drifted away. ''How come I had to get down on one knee and you don't?''

In that instant, Melanie felt the icy fear that had been lodged in her gut for two weeks melt away. She felt like herself again. She was in love with Caleb Chisholm, and he was going to marry her. Just as soon as he got his pound of flesh.

All right, then, she thought. After what she had put him through lately, he'd earned it. She lowered herself to one knee. ''Caleb Chisholm, will you marry me?''

''Say yes!'' came a shout from the back of the house.

''Say yes!'' came another from the corral.

''Say yes,'' Melanie nearly growled, ''so I can get up and go kill your brothers.''

He didn't say yes. Instead, he pulled her up into his arms with a fierce ''Come here to me.''

Melanie had feared many times in recent hours that she might never know again the feel of his arms around her. The sensation of warmth, of welcome and safety, overwhelmed her. ''Is this a yes?'' she whispered.

"This is definitely a yes." He squeezed her tightly against him.

Melanie thought she had cried herself dry during the night, but suddenly she was wracked with deep, hard sobs.

"Oh, Mel, don't cry. Please don't cry. You're tearing me up."

"I'm sorry," she sniffed. "I'm so sorry for all of this, Caleb. I love you so m-much, and I almost ran you away."

"You couldn't run me away at gunpoint," he assured her.

She sniffed again. "Honest?"

Caleb kissed the tip of her tear-reddened nose. "Honest." He kissed her cheek. "A week from Saturday, huh?"

"Is that a problem?"

"Not for me," he swore. "But I guess we better go tell our families so they can make a big fuss. Oh, and I've been told to inform you that if we need any flower girls for the ceremony, I have a couple of new nieces who have experience in that area and who would be more than willing to help us out."

Melanie laughed and hugged him. "This ought to set a few tongues wagging."

"Why's that?"

"Me, marrying you, with Sloan's daughters as my flower girls. The gossips are going to love it."

With his arms around her, he clasped his hands together at the small of her back and studied her face. "How is that gossip going to sit with you?"

"I could care less," she said airily. "I know which

Chisholm brother is the right one, and I've got him all to myself.''

"That you do." He lowered his lips toward hers and kissed her. "That, you do."

Epilogue

They were married a week from that next Saturday, in the late afternoon at the same Baptist church where only last summer Sloan and Emily had wed.

There was no large crowd this time. Melanie and Caleb hadn't wanted one, and there hadn't been time to plan for many guests anyway.

There was some gossip, as Melanie had predicted, about her not being able to make up her mind between one brother and the next. About her moving down the ladder to brother number two when brother number one was taken.

But mostly the gossip came from Alyshia Campbell.

Having become, by the virtue of saying "I do," a mature married woman, Melanie decided to be magnanimous and ignore the barracuda instead of gouging her eyes out. After all, if it hadn't been for Alyshia,

Melanie might never have kissed Caleb that night at the party.

If she hadn't kissed him, how would they have known that their worlds were not complete without each other?

* * * * *

Two brothers married—one more to go!
Look for THE COWBOY ON HER TRAIL
in August 2004 to find out who
Justin takes as his bride!

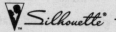

SPECIAL EDITION™

From bestselling author

VICTORIA PADE

Northbridge Nuptials

*Where a walk down the aisle
is never far behind.*

Wedding Willies

(Silhouette Special Edition #1628)

Although she's famous for bailing on two of her own
trips to the altar, Kit McIntyre has no problem being
part of her best friend's happy day. But when she's
forced to spend lots of one-on-one time with the sexy
best man, Ad Walker, Kit's eyes are finally opened
to the very real possibility of happily-ever-after.

*Available August 2004
at your favorite retail outlet.*

And coming in January 2005,
don't miss Book Three, ***Having the Bachelor's Baby.***

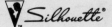

SPECIAL EDITION™

**Their word is their bond,
and their hearts are forever.**

The Cowboy on Her Trail

(Silhouette Special Edition #1632)

by

JANIS REAMS HUDSON

Rancher Justin Chisholm was completely
content with the single life—until he met teacher
Blaire Harding. After spending one night together
and becoming pregnant, beautiful Blaire suddenly
started to avoid him. Justin would do all he could
to tempt her down the wedding trail, but could
this cowboy succeed?

*Available August 2004
at your favorite retail outlet.*

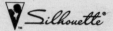

SPECIAL EDITION™

From award-winning author

MARIE FERRARELLA

Diamonds and Deceptions

(Silhouette Special Edition #1627)

When embittered private investigator Mark Banning came to San Francisco in search of a crucial witness, he didn't expect to fall in love with beautiful bookworm Brooke Moss—daughter of the very man he was searching for. Mark did everything in his power to keep Brooke out of his investigation, but ultimately had to face the truth—he couldn't do his job without breaking her heart....

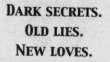

THE *PARKS* EMPIRE

DARK SECRETS.
OLD LIES.
NEW LOVES.

Available at your favorite retail outlet.